Atlanta Tully
Time Traveller

Brian Tyrer & Jane Schaffer

Illustrated by
John Lightbourne and Geraldine Mitchell

Seven Arches Publishing

Published in June 2010
By Seven Arches Publishing
27, Church Street, Nassington, Peterborough PE8 61QG
www.sevenarchespublishing.co.uk

A catalogue record for this book is available from the British Library.

Cover design, scans and typesetting by Alan McGlynn.

Printed in Great Britain by imprintdigital.net

ISBN 978-0-9556169-8-3

A big 'thank you' to the children of Years 4, 5 and 6 at Aspinal Primary School, Reddish, Manchester. Their ideas, interest and encouragement made all the difference to the production of this book.

CHAPTER 1

A Museum Just Around The Corner

'The telly's going off, Martine. And…' this word said very loudly so that the three children standing outside the bedroom door could not fail to hear, '…there's to be no more playing on that Wii. What a ridiculous name!' The children pulled faces at one another.

'They're putting their coats on and getting out into the fresh air. That way you'll get some proper rest.'

'Thanks, mum,' whispered Martine through a throat that felt as if it were lined with red-hot fiery spikes. She had a head that pounded and limbs that ached, and was too ill to get out of bed: that was why she had resorted to the drastic step of phoning her mum to ask for help. And there was the matter of her talented daughter's interview the very next day at Manchester's prestigious School of Music.

Mum, the children's nana, had come on the first bus from Prestwich. She had arrived armed with bulging carrier bags filled with shopping, which was a good thing because there was nothing left to eat in the house.

'Culture, that's what these kids need, Martine – culture. You live ten minutes walk from a whole heap of culture, and you've never even set foot in the place.'

'They've all been to the museum with the school, mum.' Martine made a feeble protest at her mum's implication of poor parenting on her part.

'Well they're going today, and you're taking this, my girl.' From out of a bulging handbag came a large bottle of Dr. Lacey's Remedy. She poured out a spoonful of the thick brown liquid and held it out for Martine to swallow. Without saying a word, Martine gulped down the proffered spoonful, grimacing.

'That'll have you better in no time. I can never understand why you don't keep a bottle of Dr. Lacey's in the house, Martine. I've told you often enough.'

Martine closed her eyes, praying that her mother would go downstairs.

'I'm going to make lunch now. You need to eat something.'

Outside in the hallway, the two younger children, Geneva and Lincoln, scurried down the stairs into the lounge to get a last few minutes of telly time before the dragon switched it off. Atlanta dodged behind her bedroom door to escape being seen. When she was sure that it was safe she came out and crossed the hall, pushing open her mother's door. She was annoyed.

'I thought you said I was doing a really good job of looking after everyone.'

'You were, sweetheart.'

'Then why did you have to phone Nana Prestwich?'

'Because there was no food in the house.'

There was no arguing with that. Atlanta had made tea the night before with the last tin of beans. The supermarket was only a ten minute walk away, but it might as well have been ten miles as far as Atlanta was concerned – she was not allowed to go out on her own in Moss Side where they lived, even in the daytime. Although in all her eleven years of life Atlanta had never seen a gunman, her dad had been shot dead by one, just a few streets away from their house – a mistaken identity shooting. Atlanta was not even one at the time. It had made her mum very cautious.

'If Travis had a proper job like Verity's dad he wouldn't be thousands of miles away, and he could look after us. He could take me for my interview.' It was, she knew, a cruel thing to say because her mum missed Travis terribly.

She banged the door as she went out, but not really badly. She went and sat on her bed in the room she shared with Geneva. She was already beginning to feel a bit mean for being cross when her mother was so poorly. Travis was Geneva and six-year-old Lincoln's dad. He worked as a DJ on a round-the-world liner. He was like a real dad to her, so she missed him too.

Atlanta sighed. She would phone Simon, the one person who almost understood her. Simon played the violin like her, and although he was not quite as much an outsider at school as she was, he still had some of her problems. Besides, he would stop her worrying about her interview tomorrow and tell her that she was the best violinist ever. She pushed her hand under her pillow. Her fingers didn't connect with her mobile. She swiped the pillow off the bed. Nothing! Nothing but a white sheet! She jumped up and dashed down the stairs and into the lounge.

'Geneva – give it to me!'

Her sister stared at her blankly.

'GIVE IT TO ME!'

'I haven't got it.'

Geneva didn't need to be told what Atlanta was asking about. There were only two things Atlanta would get so anxious about losing: her violin and her mobile. It was quite obvious it wasn't the violin because that was propped up against the music stand in the corner of the room.

'GIVE IT TO ME! Atlanta screeched again and grabbed her sister's arm, pulling her off the sofa.

'Get off me.'

'Not until you give it me.' Atlanta grabbed a handful of Geneva's bushy, black, curly hair.

'Let go!!'

Nana Prestwich appeared in the doorway. She didn't say anything, but with a firm and painful grip she propelled Atlanta out of the lounge and into the kitchen.

The lecture lasted at least half an hour. It included references to Nana Prestwich's own mother, to the agony aunt in the women's magazine that Nana Prestwich read from cover to cover each week, and to the Torah (Nana Prestwich was Jewish). Atlanta's anger morphed into boredom, and she began to despair. Then she remembered the solution: standing completely still, and with amazing skill, her face took on a tragic look, and huge round tears rolled down her cheeks.

'Oh darling, don't cry. Life's so hard, you know. I don't like being cross with you; you little ones are my life – my life.' Sniff, sob, sniff, sob. Nana Prestwich loved a good cry.

An hour later, after an early lunch, they were all on their way to the museum, which was, as Nana Prestwich had pointed out, just round the corner; well, to be more precise, round a twenty-minute-walk-away corner.

Atlanta led, striding out as if she couldn't wait to get to the museum, but in reality she was trying to get away from the cross feelings inside of her. She was still cross with mum, and now she was even more cross with Geneva. Geneva kept catching her up and giving little tugs to her coat, whispering: 'I've not taken it, honestly Atlanta, I've not,' or 'I bet you left it at Verity's yesterday. You know how you lose stuff.'

Atlanta didn't even turn round. She just walked on a little faster to escape the tugs. After about ten minutes, though, the crossness began to be edged out of her head by swirls of musical patterns, memories of whole orchestral pieces she had heard. Atlanta's feet walked, but she forgot where she was going and forgot to be cross with Geneva; she was, as she often was, drifting on a river of music inside her head. She even forgot to think about how strange it was that next year she would be going to secondary school – something she generally thought about a lot – and the fact that the next day she would be going for an interview at a school where everyone played a musical instrument. If she were successful at the interview for Chetham's School of Music, she wouldn't be the odd one out anymore.

When they got to the museum, Nana Prestwich gave her a shake.

'Atlanta, stop daydreaming.' Nana Prestwich, like all the family, was used to the times when Atlanta seemed 'out of it.' They all recognised the strange, blank look on her face. They called it daydreaming, which annoyed her, though she never said.

As she returned to reality, she realised that she would have to go through the whole business of trailing round with a six-year-old and an eight-year-old, unless she could quickly think up a way of getting out of it. They bustled into the entrance hall and stood undecided as to which way to go first.

'Nana, could I go up to the coin-collection room? We did a mini-topic on coins through the ages at school at the end of term, and it really interested me,' Atlanta lied. Geneva pulled a face at her that managed to convey both disbelief in what Atlanta was saying and good riddance.

'Atlanta, where you get your brains and talent from, I don't know.' Nana Prestwich beamed at her. If truth be known, she found her genius grand-daughter a little scary. 'Of course you can, darling. I don't think these two will find the coin collection interesting.

They'll want to see the dinosaur bones, won't you, darlings?'

'Yes, Nana, of course,' answered Geneva dutifully.

'I'm hungry,' said Lincoln.

'No, you're not,' said Nana Prestwich firmly. 'We've just had lunch. But we will go to the café later. If you all behave yourselves nicely, I'll take you for some tea in the café.'

'Tea in the café!' exclaimed Geneva, brightening up. It was very unusual for Nana Prestwich to spend any money on eating out.

'Well, I won't have time to make you anything when we get back. I shall have to go for my bus. So, just this once, we'll have tea out. You must be good, mind, and Atlanta, you must meet us at the café at…' Nana Prestwich consulted her watch '…four o'clock. That gives us an hour and a half. Have you got that, Atlanta?'

'Yes, Nana.'

'Now I can trust you to be sensible, can't I?'

'Yes, Nana.'

'And don't go talking to any strangers, especially grown ups.'

'Of course not, Nana.'

Nana Prestwich smiled. Satisfied that Atlanta was not going to meet with some unspeakable fate, she led Geneva and Lincoln in the direction of the dinosaur hall. Atlanta saw Geneva turn and give her one last reproachful look, which might have meant: 'how can you leave me to face Nana Prestwich on my own?' or, 'how can you think I've taken your mobile phone?'

CHAPTER 2

You Can Meet Some Strange People In Museums

Atlanta climbed the stairs to the room that housed the museum's coin collection. Although she had lied about her school doing a project on coins, she had not lied about her interest in them. It seemed, though, that there were not many others who shared her interest. For a good quarter of an hour she was the only person peering into the glass cases at the small, generally round objects that in bygone times had been passed from hand to hand in exchange for goods.

There was a low table in the middle of the room where children could do coin rubbings if they wished. Atlanta got a piece of paper and a pencil from the table and started making lists of the coins in one of the cases. She had just written 'silver, 1532 – that is 478 years old' when she realized that a girl, a little taller than herself, had come into the room and was now standing beside her. Atlanta tried to concentrate on the next coin, but found that she couldn't. Her mind suddenly started to fill with music – music that she knew she had never heard before. The sounds were so intense, so beautiful, she felt almost weak. She walked over to the small stools arranged around the central table and sat down. For the first time in her life, she didn't want to hear the music that was filling her head. Vaguely aware that the strange girl had followed her, she lay her head on her arms, caught between ecstatic delight and the desire for the music to stop.

'My name is Mela,' said the girl. As soon as she spoke the music stopped.

'Did you do that – fill my head with music?' Atlanta asked the question without stopping to think how strange it must sound.

'Yes,' said the girl. She had long black hair, even longer and blacker than Atlanta's. And her eyes – well, what were her eyes? Were they brown? Were they green? Atlanta found herself looking into the strange girl's eyes without hesitation.

'Why?' she managed to ask.

'Because I know you are very musical, and I thought you would like it.'

'Well, it frightened me.'

'I am sorry – I suppose it must have done. I wasn't thinking, forgive me.'

'I've never heard anything like it.'

'Of course not. It's our music. Music from the future.'

'Music from the future,' Atlanta whispered, not doubting for a moment what the girl said. That was the only explanation for the sounds she had heard.

Just then, a family came into the room. The parents went to look in one of the glass cases, and the two children sat at the small table and started doing rubbings. The strange girl was still looking at her. She got up and came round to the side of the table where Atlanta was sitting.

'Come and talk to me over there,' she said, pointing to one of the glass cases in the corner of the room. She held out a hand. Atlanta did as she was told, letting the girl lead her across the room, almost as if she were hypnotised.

'I am sorry to rush you, but I haven't much time.'

'I'm not supposed to talk to people I don't know.' Atlanta said, rather belatedly remembering her promise to Nana Prestwich.

'But you do know me, because you know my favourite music.'

'It was very beautiful – that's what scared me.'

They stood side by side at one of the cases, and the girl put her hand on the glass. Almost absentmindedly Atlanta found herself examining the girl's hand. It was slim and light-brown, almost the same colour as her own, but instead of having five fingers there were seven: six digits and a thumb; strangely, it didn't look deformed. The girl put her other hand beside it.

'Yes, you're right. I do have six fingers and a thumb; most people from our time do. It's not genetic – we have the alteration at birth.' She paused.

Atlanta opened her mouth to speak, but no words came out. Then she managed to say: 'Really?' which in no way expressed her confusion.

'As I said, I'm sorry to rush you Atlanta, but...'

Before she could carry on Atlanta butted in:

'How do you know my name? I haven't said my name.'

'Do you feel scared of me now?'

'No, but I don't know why – I should be scared – your fingers, your eyes, your knowing my name, all these things should scare me, but the only thing that has scared me was that music, and now the thought of it doesn't scare me anymore: I want to hear it again.'

'We haven't time, I'm afraid. I would love to play it again for you, but I've got to talk to you really quickly, because soon I will have to go. I've made a bit of a mess of this meeting – I do hope I won't lose any marks. This is my first trip to the twenty-first century, and I really wanted to meet you because we have so much in common.' Atlanta didn't understand any of what the girl was saying, but she didn't interrupt her. The thought flitted through her head that perhaps this was part of some strange new reality TV show, and that cameras and TV people would suddenly come in, laughing at her for taking the girl seriously; but no, that could not be – no one could create music like the music she had just heard.

'I've come to give you this back.' The girl put Atlanta's mobile on the sloping glass cover, and slowly, very slowly, it started to slip down into Atlanta's hand.

'My mobile!'

'Yes, we had to borrow it for a while. Look on the right-hand side.'

'There are three extra buttons.' Atlanta murmured.

'Exactly. Now listen carefully, Atlanta. The black button is for information. When you are alone, preferably at home, press the black button and you will be told all about SHARP 15799. I must explain what SHARP stands for: it's the Scientific History and Art Reclamation Programme, and you're on, or could be on, the fifteen thousand, seven hundred and ninety-ninth programme.' The girl paused. 'It's important you remember that number.'

'I always remember numbers: it's 15799.'

'I knew you would have no problem with that,' the girl said. 'The background to SHARP is that, with the start of the New Democracy, which replaced the Dark Chaos of the intervening years, humankind (that's everyone left on Earth now – no nationalities, just humankind) has been trying to piece together our history from the earliest of times. Unfortunately, so few records are left that we have to do it by time-travel exploration. We mainly visit the twenty-first century, which is sort of our limit. That is why we want you to travel back further in time and gather information for us.'

'You want me to travel back in time?' Atlanta heard the strange words coming out of her mouth, but somehow didn't find them strange. 'My mum doesn't even let me venture out into the neighbourhood where I live on my own, and you're saying I can go back into the past – on my own?'

The girl smiled: 'You might see people using the coins that you find so fascinating to buy actual things.'

'You're teasing me.'

'Yes, about the coins, but not about the time travel back to the past – I think you would love it. It's amazing! Truly amazing! I love being here with you – just knowing someone from a different time is the most fantastic thing.'

Atlanta understood what the girl was saying. 'It has been wonderful meeting you.'

'So you'll think about it? The black button on your phone will explain everything you need to know. My name is Mela, and I am your contact person with the future.'

'But why me, Mela, why me?'

'I chose you – it was my responsibility to choose

the person I linked up with in the twenty-first century, and I chose you because you play the violin. I am an advanced student at SHARP, but my first degree was music. The other student working like me chose his contact person for different reasons.'

'Other? Another person like me has been contacted?'

'Yes, a boy. It was decided that a student called Kazaresh – he's a nice guy, very clever – should go first with his programme (it's always the boys isn't it?) It was a great success. The boy from your time has already made two trips back in time – two very successful trips. He's a natural time traveller – quite amazing. It was because of the success of his programme that SHARP decided to go ahead with more, and I was chosen to go next, – well they had to pick a girl then, didn't they?'

'Was he from this country? I mean the boy who went back in time.'

'Oh yes, he was contacted just like you, at this museum. Currently, Manchester museum is SHARP's only base, but they are setting up others around the country. I really must be going now, Atlanta. When you are somewhere on your own, press the black button and it will explain everything.'

Atlanta could see that there was a very strange expression now on Mela's face, and somehow she seemed to be growing indistinct – further away without actually moving. But Atlanta didn't want to say goodbye to her, not yet. She needed to tell her something.

'The music was wonderful, Mela, and it's been wonderful meeting you.'

Mela was almost out of the room. She turned and smiled, and then was gone. Atlanta sat staring down at her phone. She wanted to hear that strange and beautiful music again so much. It was, she thought, like Mozart, only impossibly even more beautiful. She looked at the clock on the wall. Just two minutes to get down the stairs to the café before passing Nana Prestwich's deadline.

As she jumped down the stairs, two at a time, Atlanta plunged her mobile into her pocket. She flushed with guilt at the thought of how horrid she had been to Geneva.

CHAPTER 3

A Full Explanation Of The Scientific History And Arts Reclamation Programme

A miracle had happened. When they got home, mum was up and about. Not only that, but she looked perfectly well. She opened the door to them with a happy smile on her face.

'I'm better – I can't believe it; all the aches and pains have gone!'

They trooped in one by one off the street, everyone surprised and delighted to see her.

'You're well,' sighed Atlanta in relief.

Her mother gave her a quick, understanding smile. 'Yes, darling, no worries about tomorrow's interview.' Then Martine turned to her mother and said that her speedy recovery was all down to her; she had been wonderful taking the children out for the afternoon and letting her get a really good rest. And yet it didn't seem very likely to Atlanta that her mother had been returned to good health by four hour's rest. It seemed more like supernatural intervention, or was it intervention from the future?

Nana Prestwich beamed at her daughter's profuse thanks, but shook her head.

'No, Martine, it was that dose of Dr. Lacey's remedy that did the trick.'

'Yes, mum,' said Martine, happy to agree to anything now that she was well.

Very soon Nana Prestwich was bustling about getting ready to leave, issuing orders to the children to behave and commands to Martine not to overdo things. A taxi arrived to take Nana Prestwich home, and all the children gave her a kiss and thanked her for the afternoon. When it came to her turn, Atlanta was given a special caution.

'Now, don't let yourself down tomorrow at the interview by going off into one of those day-dreams of yours, Atlanta.' Atlanta winced, but said nothing. How she hated people saying she had 'day-dreams.'

When they were by themselves again, Martine sat on the sofa with Lincoln on one side and Geneva on the other. They settled down to watch the next round of 'X Factor.' Atlanta shook her head when her mum signalled for her to join them.

'I'm going upstairs to look through the Chetham brochure again,' she said. She escaped up the stairs as quickly as possible, whizzing into the bedroom and sitting with her back to the door, so that if anyone came in she would have time to hide her phone. She flicked it open and stared at the three new buttons down the side. She didn't know whether the uncomfortable, tight feeling inside her was because she was scared at what would happen if she pressed the black button, or whether she was worried that Geneva would come barging in.

When she pressed the black button she squeezed her eyes tight shut, so she did not see the screen sliding away from the base and expanding. No sound came from the phone. After almost a minute of sitting with her eyes shut she opened them slowly to see a large screen floating in front of her, the edges defined by a black rim. A message in black letters on the background of swirling colours read:

‹**WELCOME, ATLANTA, TO SHARP 15799**›

You can put the mobile down now. The screen will stay in place until you press the black button again.

Just as in the museum, Atlanta felt the fear drain away from her and a strange feeling of confidence come over her. She put the phone down. The message faded. Atlanta watched as the background of swirling colours, more intense than any thing she had seen before, seemed to spin off the screen into the air around her. Then the screen cleared for a moment and the following text appeared.

> This is an invitation to you to join our project. Thank you for taking the time to find out about us, and if you decide not to accept our invitation, we apologise for any inconvenience to you that might have been caused by the changes to your mobile phone. We will return it to its original state. We have contacted you because we think you are particularly suited to Project 15799, but we will quite understand if you decline to take part. Your safety is of the utmost importance to us, and in almost all respects we can guarantee that you can travel backwards in time and return to your home time zone without any ill effects whatsoever, or any danger to yourself or the people you meet on your travels. However, every activity in life can result in danger, as I am sure you are aware, and so we cannot guarantee ultimate safety.

As soon as Atlanta finished reading, the screen

faded and the next message appeared.

After you have read all of the following, think about what we are asking you to do. All the instructions and communications after this come to you from Mela, a fully-endorsed student of the University of SHARP.

Finally, we want you to know that your involvement with this project is very helpful to us, the remaining humankind of the world, and that although it will be impossible for you to understand why, you will be making a contribution to the continuance of civilisation upon earth.

Our Company Policy is: Be of good hope, and travel back in time and return in the spirit of greater good for all mankind.

The screen changed once more. This time there was a countdown, with numbers flashing on the screen so quickly it was impossible to read them until they began to slow, and then Atlanta realised it was a countdown of years. At 2010 the numbers halted and the following words appeared on the screen:

‹INSTRUCTIONS to Atlanta Tully from Mela Wang›

Hello, Atlanta. It was great meeting you at the museum. The instructions below come from me but they are standard SHARP instructions. You can ask questions by sending a text to SHARP 15799.

‹Pre-Travel Information›

When there is the possibility of a journey to a different time zone, the screen of your mobile will glow blue and you will feel a low-level vibration, different in pulse to its usual one. This may last for up to two hours your time. After that, the opportunity will have passed, but you will be sent a further opportunity.

‹Travel Information›

If you are ready to travel, make sure you are alone and somewhere where you will not be interrupted. You will be gone for between **four to six** minutes, your time. It will seem to you when you are on a time journey that you are away for much longer. It is not desirable for anyone to see you go or return, so make sure that no one is likely to be worried by your disappearance.

Wearing clothes is not helpful, so you will need to wear

something skin-tight – what you call a swimming costume is best. You will have received from us a small bag that you must wear. It doesn't need ties or anything. It is called a time/space bag. When you have taken your clothes off, press the bag to your waist, on top of any skin-tight item you are wearing. Do this BEFORE you press the button on your mobile to go. Remember, it's the green one. The bag contains a small silver disc that you must put on your forehead when you arrive. The disc is almost weightless, so you will not notice it, but it will record everything you see. It only activates when it is worn, and it only lasts a short while, so do not put it on until AFTER you arrive in the past. On your arrival, take the disc out and press it to your forehead. The backing disc will come away. Put this and your phone into the bag and secure the fastening. You'll find that the bag attaches itself to you without any discomfort. It cannot be taken from you and assures your safe return. I was wearing one in the museum when we talked.

‹Journey›

When you are ready to go, key in the project number, 15799, and press the **black** button. A screen will appear that will tell you where you are going, what you will see and whom you will meet. It identifies a Destination. Read these travel instructions very carefully, and when you are sure you have understood them, key in project number 15799 and then press the **green** button. The system will be activated and you will be transported to the time zone indicated. Near to where you arrive there will be a pile of clothes suitable for the time and place. You must put these on as quickly as possible.

The people you meet will either mistake you for someone they know or will not be surprised that a stranger is amongst them. On your journeys you will find that you can help people; this you should do. Never do anything unkind.

‹Return Journey›

When it is time for you to return, you will feel the phone vibrating. You will have to take off the clothes and leave them in a pile, preferably somewhere they cannot be seen too easily. Take the phone out of the bag, key in 15799 and press the **red** button. If you need to return because of danger before the phone vibrates, key in 15799, remove the clothes as described above and press the red button. This should only be done under real emergency conditions.

‹After Your Visit›

We will contact you after your visit to give you an assessment of how well you have done.

We will be sending you an option for travel in the next few days. If you do not take up the option for this or the next two option times, we will assume that you have decided to decline our invitation, and we will return your mobile to its original state and retrieve our travel bag.

The screen cleared, and then the words 'Goodbye for now' appeared. Atlanta sat still while the whole amazing message began to sink in. Was this really happening to her? She was just about to switch the phone off when she realised she had a text message from Simon – it read:

Gud Luk for 2moro.

She sent back: thanx.

Then Atlanta slid the mobile phone under the dressing table, but left a little corner showing. She knew that Geneva would spot it when she came up to bed, and that would give her the opportunity to tell

Atlanta off for being careless with it. She wanted to make it up to her sister for the way she had been. She went down and squeezed in next to Geneva on the sofa and said, 'I'm sorry I was so horrid today.'

CHAPTER 4

Twenty Poor Orphan Boys

The bus swung round the corner into the terminus at Piccadilly Gardens, and everyone stood up to get off. Coats were pulled in and scarves tightened against the grey day that threatened rain at any moment. Atlanta came into the city centre every Saturday to catch the bus up to Prestwich so that she could practice the piano at her nana's house, but she never got used to the noise.

Atlanta's interview at the Chetham School of Music was at two thirty. It was only one o'clock. They had come early because Atlanta had said that she wanted to see the statue of Humphrey Chetham in Manchester Cathedral before she went into the school for her audition. The music school was only a few hundred yards from the cathedral.

'Why do you want to see a statue of some old bloke from ages ago?' Geneva had asked at breakfast.

'Because if it wasn't for him there wouldn't be any school for me to go and audition at,' Atlanta had answered.

'Do you know, Atlanta,' her seriously hip sister said, 'there's no doubt about it: you are odd.'

Atlanta just said, 'I know.'

When they got to the cathedral they walked round the perimeter. The cathedral precinct, although small, was a haven of quiet amid the bustle of the city.

'It's not a grand cathedral like York or Canterbury,' said Martine, 'but how beautiful the small spires, and look at that gargoyle silhouetted against the sky.'

When they got inside they had no trouble finding the statue of Humphrey Chetham – it was across from the door they had come in by. A huge statue made of marble, it depicted Humphrey Chetham sitting on a chair, holding a roll of paper tied with a bow. At his feet was a small boy, wearing a uniform that later Atlanta learned had been worn unchanged by the 'foundationers' at the hospital school for three hundred years, until well into the twentieth century.

The sculptor had given Chetham a kind face. He had shoulder-length hair and a pointy beard, and was wearing a hat that, Atlanta thought, looked a bit like a beany. Round his neck he had a wide ruff, and a full coat went to his knees. Silk stockings were revealed on his lower legs and his high-heeled shoes were finished with buckles. The boy below the seated Sir Humphrey wore the Tudor coat sometimes known as a bluecoat.

Suddenly a voice behind them said: 'George Pilkington, the lad there with Humphrey, wine merchant 1852. That's six tons of marble there, you know.' The voice belonged to a man wearing a long black gown – someone connected with the cathedral.

'How very interesting,' Martine said, being polite.

'He was a foundationer, was George,' the man continued, obviously pleased that he had visitors seemingly eager to hear the history of the statue, 'and very successful in business in Manchester – said he owed it all to the hospital (that's Chetham's you know) for taking him in when he became an orphan. So he had the statue put there. It took a bit of damage when a bomb took out the regimental chapel in the Second World War – look at his knee, it looks as though someone tested his reflexes too hard.' He paused while Martine and Atlanta peered at the damaged knee.

'Were you in the cathedral when the bombs fell?' asked Atlanta.

The man laughed. 'I know I'm old – I've been one of the cathedral wardens for forty years – but that doesn't make me old enough to have been a warden when the bombs were falling. No, I was a young lad then, younger than you, tucked up in my bed in Higher Blackely.'

Martine looked at her watch. 'Thank you, it's been very interesting talking to you but we must be off now.'

The high boundary wall of Chetham's School of Music was just a short walk from the cathedral. They crossed the wide open space of Long Millgate, recently re-designed with low splashing fountains and seating for outdoor performances, to arrive at the school's lodge with its massive old gates and a modern, electronically operated barrier. As they approached, a porter came towards them.

'Yes, Madame – what can we do for you?'

'Atlanta Tully for an interview,' said Martine, unable to keep a hint of pride from her voice.

The man popped into the small office of the gatehouse, beckoning to them to follow him in. He picked up the phone.

'Arthur Dalton here, on the gate; there's a Miss Tully with her mother for an interview.' A short pause. 'Right, the baronial hall certainly – bit unusual that isn't it? Oh, I see, they haven't finished recording yet. OK, I'll bring them round.' He put the phone down and turned to the other man in the gatehouse. 'Bill, you mind the shop. I'm taking Miss Tully and her mum to the baronial hall.'

He led them beneath the gatehouse with its enormous wooden doors, hung on massive hinges and studded with large iron nails, and into the protected courtyard.

'Do you ever close the gates?' Atlanta asked as she drew level with the porter.

'Every night, miss,' said Dalton. 'I don't know whether it's to keep the riff raff out or to keep the riff raff in, but they're shut every night.'

Arthur Dalton was going at a good pace, and Martine, smartly dressed in a black suit with a tight skirt and elegant black high-heels, was struggling to keep up. Suddenly the heel of her shoe caught in a cobble. She wobbled desperately and let out a loud 'ow…ouch' as her ankle twisted over. Atlanta turned to help her.

'I bet Humphrey Chetham had trouble on these cobbles as well,' said Atlanta, much to the surprise of Arthur Dalton.

'Why do you say that, miss?'

'Well, the statue of him in the cathedral has him wearing high heels.'

'Not as high or as silly as mine,' said Martine, giving a little laugh as she regained her composure.

'My fault for going too fast.'

'Oh no, not at all,' Martine smiled at him.

They went more slowly after that, and followed a path that ran alongside the building. They had time to notice that the ancient medieval house was made from massive stone blocks, some a soft pink colour, perhaps replacing ones that over the centuries had become too worn.

'So when did you see the statue in the cathedral?' asked Arthur Dalton.

'We've just been there. I wanted to see what Humphrey Chetham looked like before I came to the school.'

'Interested in the history of the place, then, are you?'

'Oh yes. Isn't everyone?'

'Not as you'd notice. Well, that path leading away down there is called the long path, and we've just walked along the top flat. That passage over there is the bell passage, and it leads into the pump court where they used to pump water up from the Irk. Wouldn't want to drink the water nowadays! Used to brew beer with it back in Tudor times. Today we have

CHAPTER 5

A River Of Music

Arthur Dalton pushed the heavy door open for them and they stepped into a small, dark hallway with a sign saying 'To the Library' pointing up a wooden stairway. To the left, an arched doorway led on to a dark corridor. Sounds of footsteps hurrying down the corridor towards them were followed by the appearance of a tall man in a long black gown. He stopped, rather out of breath, and said:

'Ah, Dalton, this will be Miss Tully no doubt.' He gave them a warm, welcoming smile. Despite his height and flowing gown, he wasn't imposing.

'Yes, Dr Smallwood,' Dalton replied. Then, turning to Atlanta and Martine, he said: 'This is Dr Smallwood.'

'Percival Smallwood, at your service.' The man gave a mock bow, twirling one hand a little above his head as he did so. Atlanta grinned, and Martine said:

'Very pleased to meet you.' They shook hands.

'The pupils call me Percy – we don't stand on ceremony here. But this morning we are a little disarranged and somewhat behind schedule, so I am going to have to ask you to wait for a short while. Is that alright, Atlanta?'

'Oh yes, perfectly alright.'

'The hall is being used, but we can go in and listen if you like; a young man is performing his own composition. Would you like to hear it?'

'Very much,' Atlanta replied. She had already caught the drifting sounds of a piano, and the river of colours was starting to run through her head.

'Excellent,' said Dr. Smallwood. 'Dalton, would you be so good as to take Mrs Tully to the refectory and find a cup of tea for her?' He turned to Martine. 'You don't mind, do you? But we like to talk to prospective students on their own.'

Martine, wondering what a refectory was, quickly reassured him that she didn't mind, though one look at Atlanta's face made her worry: she could see that Atlanta was getting her 'spaced-out' look on her face.

'Follow me, then, Mrs Tully,' said Dalton, turning back the way they had come. 'I think we might persuade the cook to release some of the cakes that she has made for the Feoffees' tea later today.'

That jolted Atlanta back to the present. 'The

who?' she asked – the place was full of unknown and peculiar words!

'The Feofees,' explained Dalton, 'are the committee that's been running the place since the executors of Humphrey Chetham's will bought it back in 1653.'

Atlanta gave Martine a small wave goodbye and then followed Dr. Smallwood down a long, dark corridor that could easily have been a Hogwarts corridor. On one side, small arched windows cut into the thick stone walls let in light from an enclosed courtyard. On the other wall were narrow wooden doors, tightly shut. What dark mysteries did they conceal? They came to a large door that blocked the end of the corridor, and the person playing the piano was obviously on the other side, as now the music was quite loud.

'We have to wait whilst the staff make an evaluation of one of our senior pupils' work,' said Dr. Smallwood in a hushed voice. 'He's called Keith Francis, and it is proposed that we enter him in the Vienna – that's a prestigious competition for young pianist composers. The candidates have to play a work of their own, and they also play two other set pieces. It's in Vienna, of course, and the winner is assured a glittering future as well as a very lucrative recording deal. But anyway, we will go in and just listen, shall we?' He looked down at the small, rather chubby girl by his side. Would she have even half the talent of Keith, he wondered. The piano music stopped.

Dr. Smallwood lifted a finger to his lips, indicating the need for quiet, and pushed the door open slowly. Even though he took great care, it made a creaking noise. Almost on tiptoes, Atlanta followed Dr. Smallwood into the enormous space of the baronial hall. Great black beams supported the ceiling; the walls were bare stone and the floor was covered with massive slabs worn smooth by the passing of feet over the centuries. Portraits of stern-faced men and women glowered down from the walls at them, and over the massive fireplace was a bust of Humphrey Chetham himself.

The pianist began again. The piece lasted about fifteen minutes, and when it was completed the two adults went over to Keith and shook his hand. There was a bit of chatting, all very jolly, and then Keith thanked them, shut the lid of the grand piano and left.

'They will have to think about this because it's the first time he has played for them,' said Smallwood, 'and of course they will want to compare notes before they report back, and before they make their recommendations to the director of music.'

'Who is the director of music?' asked Atlanta.

'Me,' smiled Smallwood. 'But I know the boy, and I really want an objective opinion, which is why the two you saw were here...I take it you didn't recognise them?'

'No,' said Atlanta, wishing she could say 'yes'. For the first time that day she began to feel a little worried: would her lack of knowledge of the world of classical music go against her? Everyone was expecting her to do well; it would be awful to fail. 'Will it make a difference, my not knowing famous pianists?'

'Oh no, that doesn't come in to it all, don't you start worrying now. Anyway, now we have the place to ourselves let me explain. As you know, this is the first round, and if you get beyond that you will be invited back to be interviewed by our specialist string people. We'll see how it goes, shall we?' Dr Smallwood walked over to where there were some wooden seats set either side of a table.

'We can sit out of the way over here. This is the ladies' bay, and it's supposed to be where, in olden days, when a fight broke out in the hall, all the ladies would go in order to be safe – the rule was that no one could harm anyone who was in here. So we should be quite safe, eh?' They sat down. 'Sorry about the delay, but in any event it gave you the opportunity to see and hear what some of our best pupils can do by the time they are ready to go forth into the world. Very good, wasn't it?'

'Yes… but...' The 'but' popped out of her mouth before she could stop it. It hung in the air, small and prickly. She shouldn't have said the 'but,' and she realised that at once by the change in Dr Smallwood's expression. Up until then he had beamed and smiled at her. Now he looked almost angry.

'But what?' There was a sharp tone to his question.

'Well,' began Atlanta slowly, and feeling for the first time a terrible churning in her stomach – she had definitely blown it now; there was nothing she could do but carry on and try and explain to this tall, now stern-looking man what she had heard in her head. 'At first I thought his piece was really good: I… I don't know many musical words,' she stuttered, 'but to me I could see that the music was flowing well but then came some wrong colours – colours that dragged it down.'

'Wrong colours?' questioned Smallwood. He still looked stern, but slightly less angry. 'That's an interesting way of describing musical composition – but just what does it mean?'

Atlanta felt her mouth go dry. 'It's difficult to describe – I see things – words, numbers, sounds – in colour. Like a river, but not just the surface of the river, all the way down to the bottom, with rocks and deep bits and then with fish and animals and sunshine and wind. It's difficult to explain, but I can show you if you like.'

'How can you show me?' asked Smallwood.

'Let me play what I heard on the piano and I'll show you where I would change the piece.'

'This I have got to hear,' said Smallwood. Fortunately, Atlanta didn't realise that there was deep sarcasm in his voice. Dr. Smallwood was now convinced that Atlanta was probably deluded. How did this strange child come to be granted an interview at all? She obviously had some real problems; the interview would soon be over. He was so glad that he would not have to report back to her mother the outcome – that would be done by a formal letter by his secretary. He sighed; for some reason he had taken to this girl and had hoped she would be OK.

Atlanta had to ask Smallwood to help her open the lid of the piano, as it was so heavy, and then had to ask for more help in adjusting the stool so that she could reach the pedals. When she was ready, Smallwood said:

'I don't remember reading that you were a pianist on your application form?'

'No,' replied Atlanta. 'My teacher said not to put it on the form because I've not had any lessons.' She didn't say any more, but started to look down at the keys of the piano very intently, just as she always did when she played the piano at her nana's house.

Dr Smallwood had gone to sit down, dreading the thought of what he was about to hear. Whatever made this strange girl think that she could play Keith's piece? She had only heard it once. Of course, it would just be a jumble of notes, perhaps a few chords that she could pick out by ear. He sat despondently – he had listened through numerous pieces played by interviewees that were not up to scratch, but this one would surely take the cake.

Atlanta started playing. She began tentatively.

Dr. Smallwood recognised the piece immediately. Not note perfect, it was nevertheless unmistakably the opening bars of Keith's composition! His face went white. Atlanta played for about five minutes, then stopped and said:

'This is what he did here,' and she played a few more bars, then said, 'but this is what I would have done.'

When she had finished, Smallwood took the top off a bottle of water that had been on the table, filled a glass and drank its contents down in one. He was now very white and shaking.

'Are you alright?' asked Atlanta.

'Yes, I'm alright,' Dr Smallwood squeaked. He tried to calm himself down, reminding himself that he was with an eleven-year-old child. He knew he had seen a small miracle: what Atlanta proposed as an alternative to the section in question was, without doubt, infinitely better. He rushed over to the table where Francis had left his music and opened it at random. Leaning over Atlanta, he struck some notes that were part of the piece. 'Can you carry on from there?'

'Yes,' said Atlanta and she did.

Smallwood collapsed back onto the bench.

'You memorised a piece of music for an instrument that is self-taught, and just played it! How?'

'Like I said, it's a river, and I go in the river, and it moves, and I move with it. I can see a pattern, and then the patterns stay in my head. It's like… like numbers really.'

Smallwood was still white and sweating. 'Have you done this before?' he asked.

'What, with the piano? No,' said Atlanta.

'But why didn't you mention this in your application?' said Smallwood.

'Well…' said Atlanta, 'my experience is that if you are different then people don't like it and they are nasty to you – that's why I wanted to come here, because I knew everyone was a brilliant musician and so they wouldn't be against me.'

'If only that were true,' sighed Smallwood. 'People will always be jealous. And this place is probably no different. I can't offer you a place here and now, but I think you should come here. We haven't even played the violin yet, but I don't think I can take any more in at the moment – will you come back in a few weeks' time?'

'Yes, of course,' said Atlanta.

'I'll come and tell your mother now that I definitely want you to come to Chetham's, but you'll have to go through the process in the usual way.'

'OK,' said Atlanta and smiled up at Dr. Smallwood, who felt as if he were looking at an angel.

CHAPTER 6

Getting Ready

Atlanta knew that her mum was happy because all the way home on the bus she kept telling her how proud she was of her, and that the very nice Dr. Smallwood seemed to think she was some sort of a musical genius, a child that needed special attention – special care.

Martine had always known Atlanta was especially gifted, but she had never thought about what that might mean, and she never treated her any differently to Geneva and Lincoln. She had often thought that the huge talent of Atlanta's father had lived on in his daughter; now she knew that Atlanta was even more musically talented than Anthony had been, and it was a little frightening. Not that Atlanta seemed bothered at all; she just smiled every time Martine praised her or asked her to tell her about the piano recital one more time. How calmly she's taking it all! Martine thought – I don't think she's even sent Simon a text message.

'Aren't you going to text Simon?'

'Mmm, in a minute.' Atlanta did want to text Simon but couldn't because her phone was vibrating with a pulse she'd never felt before. She guessed that it was a signal from SHARP. It had started the moment they got on the bus. She desperately wanted to look at her phone and press the black information button, but didn't dare in case the screen enlarged and detached itself from her phone the way it had done the first time a message had come through from them. That would be disastrous – her mum and all the rest of the people on the bus would be totally freaked out! Atlanta just sat still, wondering how long SHARP would keep sending the signal.

The phone was still vibrating when they got home, but there was no way Atlanta could slip away and find somewhere on her own.

Even though she'd not been texting, her mum had: neighbours, friends and, of course, Nana Prestwich had all been told of Atlanta's success, and they started arriving at the house one after the other. The doorbell kept ringing, and in would come another smiling face, another person hugging Atlanta and telling her that she was a genius.

Geneva and Lincoln began to get giddy, charging up and down the hall and running out on the pavement shouting: 'Atlanta's going to be famous.' Soon the kitchen and lounge were crowded with people congratulating Atlanta and coaxing her to play for them. She played 'Humeresque' by Dvorak and everyone clapped, and Uncle Ross, her father's brother, clapped the loudest and shouted 'Encore,' and so she played some more: another classical piece, and then her adaptations of pop songs. At some point in the evening Atlanta realised her phone had stopped pulsing. Someone had bought champagne, and with the sound of the cork popping a proper party got under way – a proper West Indian, Moss Side party that would swing and laugh into the night. Food arrived, cans of beer and bottles of wine and more and more people.

When Atlanta finally went to bed, she fell asleep immediately, but in the morning the first thing that came into her head was the thought that Mela had been trying to contact her. As she got dressed for school she wondered if SHARP might try contacting her at school – what would she do? Well, there were certainly places to which she could slip away unnoticed at school. But she would have to be ready. She went to her drawers and rifled around until she found her black swimming costume, and tucked it into her bag. Then she got out her secrets box from under her

wich, where she would spend the day practicing on the piano. As the bus wound its way up the Cheetham Hill Road, Atlanta felt the now familiar vibration of her phone. It's very strange, they always catch me on the bus, thought Atlanta, but this time I'm quite lucky. Usually, as soon as she got to her nana's house, Nana would go out, clutching her basket and her re-useable Tesco carrier bags for her weekly shop.

After saying 'hello,' Atlanta settled down at the old upright in the front room and started playing scales, just like she did every Saturday. Today, though, she felt her fingers tremble with excitement, tripping her up and causing loads of mistakes, none of which her nana noticed. Then she started worrying: supposing for some reason Nana didn't go shopping today? She would miss her second chance, and there were only three chances. But it wasn't long before she heard the familiar sounds of Nana getting herself ready to go out.

'Goodbye, Atlanta darling, I'm off to Tesco – I won't be long.'

Atlanta paused in her playing: 'Goodbye, Nana,' she called, and rippled off a particularly impressive and difficult scale. The front door banged shut.

As soon as she was sure her nana was not going

to bob back for some forgotten tokens, she stopped playing, picked up her school bag containing the swimming costume, and dashed upstairs to the bathroom, locking the door behind her. The phone was still vibrating. She pressed the black button. The screen slid away from the mobile as before, but this time it only enlarged to around the size of an exercise book.

The message read:

Hello, Atlanta. We are so pleased that you have decided to travel with us. Here are the details of your current travel options.

‹Time zone›
June 1631

‹Place›
Northern England – the centre of the town of Manchester

‹Landing›
Adjacent to target structure

‹Instructions›
Take nearest set of steps up from the riverbank and

go through into the courtyard. Then wait

‹Destination›

The building known at that time as the College of Priests, belonging to the wealthy Stanley family

‹Identity›

Henry Butterworth, a young boy who has been sent by his mother to be taken care of by the warden of the College of Priests

‹Conditions›

Favourable – weather benign – no pestilence or illness – generally stable but some threat to others from political and military action

‹Equipment›

Mobile phone, travel bag. Mobile phone fitted with beam of light activated when t-o-r-c-h is keyed in (only use sparingly)

If you wish to travel, do as follows:

› take off your clothes, except for underpants
› press the time/space travel bag close to your body so that it is attached; key in 15799

› press the green button.

Have a good trip.

Atlanta read the instructions over and over until she was sure she knew them off by heart. She quickly took off her clothes and put them in a neat pile. She got her swimming costume out of the bag and struggled into it. She pressed the time/space bag against the costume where her tummy was and, sure enough, it stuck there as if it had been glued. She gave it a little tug: it didn't shift at all.

She picked up her phone. Excitement mixed with fear made her fingers tremble, but she dialled 15799, paused for a moment, then shut her eyes and pressed the green button. She heard a faint, far-off, high-pitched whine, coming nearer and nearer, filling her ears. Then…Nothing.

CHAPTER 7

Newly Orphaned

A slight jolt. Atlanta opened her eyes. She was standing quite close to a small river of clear, fresh water. There were no sounds at all except for the slight hum from insects in the reeds that lined the river-banks. Her legs felt wobbly, so she sat down on the grass. There was a sudden flash of wings across the water as a bright green and orange bird darted from a small willow tree on the opposite bank.

She was definitely feeling the strange wooziness that Mela had warned her about. Try as she might, she couldn't remember what she was supposed to do next. So she stared at the river's clear, sparkling surface. The bird made another appearance; this time diving from a high branch of the willow into the water and back up again, a small fish in its beak. Atlanta was amazed.

Then slowly, slowly her thoughts began to clear. Without realising it, she was coming out of time-slip, and quickly. She remembered that she had to do something with the time/space bag. She felt inside and there was the small round disc. She took it out and pressed it to her forehead. The film on the disc seemed to melt into her skin, leaving only the metal base in her hand. As she had been instructed, she put this and the mobile into the bag and snapped it shut.

To her left, and in the shadow of a large flat rock, she saw a rough woollen sack. Were her clothes in there? The sack, bound with a thin leather thong that took her a minute or two to undo, smelt of something she couldn't identify – but it wasn't pleasant!

She tipped the clothes out on to the ground and picked up a pair of short woollen trousers. 'These are like those things mum calls pedal pushers,' she exclaimed out loud. She put them on, never doubting for a moment that they would fit. They did, but they were really itchy and she struggled to fasten them at the waist – no zippers or clips, just a strange wooden buckle. Next she put on a pair of long grey socks. She tucked them into the band at the bottom of the trousers. That held them up, but they wrinkled dreadfully. Then there was a white shirt – well, an almost white shirt – probably made of a coarse linen, and the outfit was completed with the addition of a short leather waistcoat. Quite smart, thought Atlanta, but the shoes! They were terrible – worn, dirty and old. Atlanta grimaced as she stuck her feet into them, and then started to giggle, thinking what Geneva would say if she could see her dressed like this!

She poked into the bottom of the sack to make sure it was empty and found a short strip of black material, fraying slightly at the edges. She used it to tie her hair back at the nape of her neck.

Once dressed, Atlanta took a look at her surroundings. Behind her rose a high sandstone wall, beyond which she could see the rooftops of a large building. Nearby, a set of stone stairs led away from the river bank, as did a similar set some 50 metres further downstream.

She set off up the steps until she came to a narrow gap in the wall. She squeezed through and emerged into a wide courtyard. She knew at once where she was. She was at the front of Chetham College. But now there were no hurrying students, no parked cars, no sound of traffic or other city noises, just a wide cobbled space with a water pump next to a stone trough. The building itself, with its deep-set windows and large blocks of mellow sandstone, was just as she had seen it only a few days before. Away across on the other side of the courtyard she could see through a tall archway the outline of a small, stone-built church. Was that small church St Mary's, the one that eventually became the huge building that was Manchester Cathedral? It must be.

The instructions had told her to walk towards the walls and go into the courtyard and wait. She'd done that. The problem was, what did she do now? She looked down at her worn-out, shabby shoes and kicked a stone, watching it bounce across the hardened earth. She kicked another, then another, each time sending the stone a little further.

'Now then, young lad, no need for such idle amusement.'

Atlanta turned quickly and saw that a man, small in stature and slightly bent, had come out of one of the passageways that led into the college, and had walked so softly over the cobbles towards her that she had not heard him. She didn't know what to say, so she just looked down as if sorry for her stone kicking. By this time he had reached her, and, to her surprise, placed a hand on her shoulder. His wrinkled brown face came close to hers, so close she could smell his bad breath! He had a friendly face, but his teeth were all black!

'Let's tek a look at ye, Henry Butterworth.' He pushed Atlanta a little way away from him. 'Me eyes do not deceive me, ye are just the teking of your father, dark as the black horse in me stables, poor man, God rest his soul. For his sake, we are teking you in, Henry. He was a good man and the best of masons – why, the roof of St Mary's is secure because of his skill. But, God save his soul, to fall from such a height!' The man stopped speaking and shook his head silently.

Atlanta, realising what the sad look on his face must mean, once more looked down at the ground and thought it best to look sad as well. Then the strange thought flickered through her mind that she and Henry Butterworth, the person whose space she was now in, both had fathers who had died accidentally.

'But no use us standing here mourning, that time is over for ye now, Henry. Ye must try to do yer very best with your lessons here, and ye will mek yeself as useful as ye can here to me and me good wife.'

'Most willingly I will.' Atlanta responded.

Then another change came over the old man. He dropped his voice to almost a whisper, as if sharing a secret. 'Ye know that there is talk of the place changing hands. There is no way there are going to be priests here again, and the Stanleys what own the place have many another fine property.' He looked at Atlanta as if expecting an answer.

'Well, I never knew any of this,' she answered truthfully.

'Well, I can tell you, Henry Butterworth, that arrived here this very afternoon, there is a most worthy gentleman come to see over with the purpose of buying it for his-self. He has gone up to the audit room with his estate manager. Now what do you think of that?'

Goodness, what should I think of that? Atlanta wondered. The old boy really was quite a gossip. Just as when kids at school told her some 'hot gos' and she had no idea why it was so interesting, she pretended great interest and amazement.

'I am most taken aback!' she exclaimed.

It seemed to be the right answer because her companion became even more animated, and lowered his voice so much that, despite the smelly breath, Atlanta had to bend near to him to hear.

'Our visitor this afternoon is none other than the gentleman of much means from Turton – Mr. Humphrey Chetham.'

'My goodness!' This time Atlanta's surprise was genuine.

'Well may ye be surprised. Why, this very afternoon, newly come from yer humble home, ye will meet with one whose business has flourished so that he is the talk of not only Manchester but the great town of Salford as well! So ye can see what opportunities might lay ahead of ye. Ye can help me to tek up provisions now. I will show ye the brew house and ye must draw a quart of ale. I'll get me to the kitchen for some victuals that my good wife is at this very moment preparing.'

In the brew house the warden, for that was who he was, showed Atlanta where the large earthenware jugs were kept, and then scurried off to the kitchen, assuming that she would know how to draw the beer. Fortunately, it was not that difficult to work out what to do. There was a small stool under the tap of one of the wooden barrels; she stood the jug on the stool and turned on the tap. Beer gushed out, frothing and foaming on the top. She went to the doorway and waited for the warden's return. Soon the old chap came scurrying towards her. He gave her a wink to follow him.

They went across the front of the building, just as on the day of her interview, and then into the great hall. Immediately she recognised it as the vast room where she had played the piano for Dr. Smallwood: there were no portraits on the walls, but otherwise it had hardly changed. They crossed the stone flags to the large oak door of the Audit Room.

'Place t'jug on the floor, Henry, and knock for us

to enter,' said the warden in a low voice. She knocked. After a moment or two there was a grinding sound as the large metal door-handle turned.

The door swung open, and a man, his hand still on the door-handle, looked straight into Atlanta's eyes. His clothes were much finer than those of the warden. He wore a blue velvet coat and a stiff lace ruff at his neck, and on his shoes were large silver buckles. But it was the way he stood and, most of all, his gaze that told Atlanta he was a man of importance and wealth. Although not really resembling his cold, white, marble statue that had frozen him in the same position for so many years, Atlanta knew at once she was looking at Humphrey Chetham. She nearly dropped the jug of beer!

Then she heard the warden say, 'We have brought you refreshment, sire.'

'So I see – put it on the table, man, before this young lad drops his jug. He looks sorely in need of refreshment himself. Is this the lad you told me about? The one whose father met with an untimely end in pursuit of his duties as a stonemason of some repute?'

'Aye, Mr Chetham. This is the very lad. His name is Henry Butterworth.'

'Very good, very good.'

Atlanta followed the warden towards a large table, and was glad to place the jug down next to the warden's two plates of meat. A great many papers were scattered about on the table, and Mr. Fielding, the estate manager, was busy writing. In his hand was a quill, the end of which had been dipped into an inkbottle. In front of him, several sheets of parchment were covered with lines of evenly shaped, sloping script.

'Join us if you would, warden. There're a few queries I have to put to you. Mr. Fielding and I have been looking through the papers and there is much I need to ask.'

The warden drew a chair up to the table. Atlanta, wondering what to do next, spotted some wooden tankards on a shelf. She poured the beer into three of them and took them to the gentleman. They thanked her with a nod. Then she noticed a stool in the corner of the room and sat down.

A clock ticked in the corner of the room, and the voices of the men droned above her head. Although there was no reason for it, Atlanta felt happy, completely at home, as if she had always lived in a place with oak-panelled walls, a decorated ceiling and arched windows cut into strong stone walls.

CHAPTER 8

Unwanted Callers

After a while, Humphrey Chetham turned and beckoned Atlantic to come to the table. She went over and stood at his side.

'So, young man, the warden here tells me that your father had great plans for you to get a good education and then to go into trade.'

'Yes, sir.'

'A man after my own heart: I place a high value on schooling. I myself went to the grammar school set up by the kind charity of Bishop Oldham, but I had a father to pay for my lessons. You are going to try to carry out your deceased father's wishes, even though you must rely on the goodwill of others. The Stanleys are unlikely to need this house, and the kind warden here is no young man; if his patronage fails you, you may have to earn a living some other way before your education is done.' Humphrey Chetham was looking solemn.

'I will work my hardest for those who help me,' said Atlanta. She suddenly realised that Henry Butterworth, unlike her and every British child in the twenty-first century, had no free state-school to go to. We just take it all for granted, she thought, even though the teachers were always telling them about places in Africa, India and other parts of the world where children are too poor to go to school.

At that moment, Mr Fielding, who had gone over to look out of the mullioned windows that overlooked the gatehouse, gave a short, sharp gasp.

'Look, sire, the King's men!' he exclaimed, and beckoned Chetham over. All four of them clustered round the window. Coming through the gate were a couple of cavalrymen and about a dozen pikemen. The horsemen were a magnificent sight. They wore wide-brimmed hats with the plumes of some exotic bird flowing over the brim. Their coats, trousers and thigh boots were leather, and across one shoulder was flung a colourful sash. Atlanta saw that they had long swords at their sides.

The pikemen looked evil, Atlanta thought. They carried the traditional sixteen-foot pike with its sharp metal spike at the end.

The warden turned and hurried across the room to the door. 'I must get to the gatehouse to speak to these men. Henry, stay here with Mr. Chetham.'

through the hall lest I be followed, so I descended to the river and came up the scurvy court steps, through the fish court, and so arrived here. Ye are in great danger, Mr Chetham. The soldiers are the King's men, and they say they have intelligence that ye are here. They went to Clayton Hall, where the housekeeper told them ye had come here and met with Mr Fielding. I have told them that ye are not yet arrived, and that only Mr. Fielding is here, but they are not in the mood to believe me. They are just holding back from a search because I mentioned the displeasure of the Lord Derby if his premises were treated thus. I don't know for how long they will hold back. They say that when ye are caught they will take ye to the palace at Westminster, for ye have displeased His Majesty. How can this be?'

'It's a long story,' muttered Chetham. 'As you know, the King finds it hard to have his way with parliament – more strength to them – and he needs to swell his coffers, for he is near penniless. He means to sell preferences to those with money, and so I am offered a knighthood – at a price. I had let it be known that I will not pay for such a thing. I did not become wealthy through trade to squander my money on titles that not only earn nothing but cost me into the bargain. I must get away from here and return to Turton where I will be safe. There is no love for the King or his men up there.

'But ye are truly snared here,' said the warden. 'The pikemen will have ye as soon as they lay eyes on ye, and if you run, either the horse or the ball from the matchlock's firearm will stop ye.'

'Is there no way out the back to the riverbank?'

'The officer has sent his men to all the doorways on the outside wall. By now they will be along the river for sure.'

'Then I am done for.'

'There is just one chance.' The old man paused as if the chance he was thinking of was not much of one. 'There's the tunnel, though there is no knowing if the way is still clear.'

'What tunnel? Tell me, man!'

'The opening to the tunnel is found half way down the wall of the well. It is not easy to see from above, but there is a small doorway that gives way if given a good kick. Then ye are in a small but passable passageway that leads on through another door until eventually ye arrive in the crypt of the church.'

'My goodness, what a risky endeavour! How did this tunnel come about?'

'They say it was dug by the de la Warre family as

a precaution against those who would sack the church and kill the clergy. It was used to save much of the plate when King Henry's men came for it. They took some, but most was brought back here safe and in secrecy.' The old man suddenly turned round and took hold of Atlanta's hand to draw her forward.

'If ye try the tunnel, ye'll need this young lad here to help.'

'Why is that, my good man?'

'Because at one point there's a door that'll only open from t'other side. Between the rock wall and the doorpost there is a small space that only a little'un can squeeze through. Then he can open the door for ye to pass through. Ye, sire, would never get through that space.'

'I see. So I will need Henry Butterworth to accompany me. Will you do that, lad?'

No one waited for Atlanta to answer. They just seemed to take it for granted that she would do whatever it was that they were planning for her. The warden remarked that Henry would be just the lad for the job because he had been a nimble helper to his dad on the roofs of the town.

But Atlanta was not Henry Butterworth! She was terrified of heights – they made her feel sick. When she was little, Martine used to have to rescue her from the platform at the top of the slide; Atlanta would be stuck there, petrified, with a queue of impatient children waiting behind her.

'Come, we must get out of here and down the cloisters; the well is in a small courtyard close by.' The warden was already opening the door and leading the way. 'But we must be quick; there's no telling how long it will be before the King's men get impatient.' The old man, still holding Atlanta's arm, led the way down the cloisters to the small, inner stone courtyard.

In the middle of the court was the open hole of the well. A heavy stone cover, wooden buckets and several lengths of rope lay around on the pebbled floor. Over the well hung a bucket on a rope wound round a pulley, with a handle on a sturdy wooden structure. The three men stood right at the edge of the open well and looked down the dark hole at the water far below. To one side, slightly above the water level, you could just make out the outline of a wooden door, if you knew what to look for.

Atlanta shivered. Peering down into the murky hole she shrank back, imagining tumbling down and falling into the black water at the bottom. She felt her mouth filling with icy water and her fingers finding no hold on the sheer, slimy walls of the well. She would drown!

It became clear to her that the plan was for the bucket to be untied from the rope that would then be tied round her waist, and for the men to lower her down first. She would have to swing on the rope in order to kick open the door. Then she was to untie the rope, and the men would pull it back up so that they could then lower Chetham down. As they explained the plan, Atlanta felt her mouth go dry with fear.

'Now, lad, that's all simple, isn't it?' the old warden asked her. Once again she didn't answer, and once again no one noticed, so busy were they in getting on quickly with their plans.

The warden hurried away in order to get a lantern, and also reinforcements for the job of lowering down the heavy man. While he was gone, Chetham and Fielding began talking about how to get a horse from Fielding's lodgings so that Chetham could make a quick escape once he had got through the tunnel to the church.

'I'll try to get a lad to take it and tether it to the church post,' said Fielding.

Atlanta knew she would have to make a run for it. She couldn't go down that well! She couldn't; it was impossible. She slipped her hand under her leather jerkin and felt the outline of the space bag with the precious mobile in it.

If she just slipped it out and pressed in the numbers, following the emergency procedures, she would be back home safely in the twenty-first century. It was an emergency: she couldn't…she just couldn't go down that black hole! She edged away from the two men so that she was only a step or two away from the cloisters. The men, talking animatedly, didn't notice.

She was just about to run when a dreadful thought came to her. If she went, they would think that it was Henry Butterworth who had run away. His name would be blackened. The old man would despise him and throw him out. He would wander the streets penniless. His father had just died and he had nowhere to go. She, Atlanta, would ruin his life! She froze to the spot. The next minute the warden came hurrying back, bringing with him another man, a rough-looking sort. He was the servant who usually drew the water from the depths of the well.

CHAPTER 9

The Tunnel

Altanta hardly noticed what was happening to her now. The rope was tied tightly round her waist, and somehow she managed to walk to the edge of the well. The men lowered her slowly down into the darkness. As always when she was frightened, Atlanta closed her eyes tight shut. The fear was so intense she thought she was going to black out, but she clung on to the rope above her head, its roughness on her hands the only thing she noticed. Then voices from above started to ricochet around the walls of the well.

'Ye'r there Henry, the door's right there at yer side.'

'Whack the door, lad!'

'Give it a kick!'

'Swing out, Henry lad, swing out so you can give the door a kick.'

She opened her eyes and saw the door just there as she hung suspended over the dreadful water. She realised that the door was now her only way to safety. She gave it a push. It didn't budge. She leant back, and the rope began to swing. She got the momentum going and this time managed a kick. Again it didn't budge. She pulled back and swung towards the door with as much strength as she could find, feet hammering against the wooden panels, again and again. Suddenly, it gave way, and the men watching above carefully played out more rope so that she landed with a heavy bump on the stone floor on the other side of the door. She got out, and with shaking fingers undid the rope. She called out, 'Pull up the rope; I'm through the door.'

The warden's voice echoed down: 'Well done, Henry Butterworth.'

And Atlanta found herself smiling in the darkness – 'I did it! I did it!' she said over and over to the rocky walls. There was a terrible, dank, musty smell, and the thought of rats crossed her mind, but she didn't care, the fear had gone.

She couldn't see what was behind her, but looking up from the doorway she could just see that Humphrey Chetham was on his way down. He held a lantern in one hand, though it wasn't lit.

'Ahh, Henry, am I here yet?' called Chetham as he swung into the doorway, holding the lantern high so as not to risk damaging it. He quickly undid the rope around his waist, and someone from above pulled it up. With that, all traces of them were gone from the courtyard above – and any chance of returning the way they had come.

'Struth it's dark! We were going to light the lantern up there, but noises told us that the King's men were inside the building, and so Fielding and the warden had to leave quickly. Only the servant stayed to do his usual task of drawing water, so nothing suspicious about that. Here, let me find my flint,' and he rummaged about in his pockets. 'Good. Now you take the lantern. Hold open the lantern gate and prepare the wick to receive the flame.' After a couple of sharp striking noises and then some sparks, Atlanta saw a small flame erupt from the box that Chetham held in his trembling hands. How wonderful the small golden flame seemed in the darkness!

Within a few seconds, Chetham had the lantern alight, with its window shut against drafts that would otherwise have blown it out.

'Well, lad, we must make our way forward now. Heaven knows what is in store for us.'

As they went forward, the tunnel became very narrow, roughly cut through the native sandstone. Small stalactites of some chemical or other hung from the roof. The air was dank but surprisingly warm.

'Well, at least we'll not perish from cold, whatever else may be in store for us,' said Chetham.

'Yes, sire, it's as warm down here as in the fresh air.'

'Ah, to be in the fresh air! How are you lad? Are you afraid?'

Startled by this direct question, Atlanta couldn't stop herself from being truthful.

'Not now, sire, but I was.'

'How's that then Henry?'

'The warden had it wrong. I have never helped my father on the roofs. I have always feared heights. I know not why it is so. I was stricken with fear as I descended the well.'

'Now I can tell you, Henry, that is something we share. I too cannot stomach heights – I was full of fear descending the well.'

Atlanta remembered that in the light of the flame from the tinderbox she had noticed his hands had been trembling.

At the start of the tunnel Mr. Chetham could stand upright, but after a few yards he had to bend down as the roof got lower and lower. They walked very slowly; Atlanta went first carrying the lantern. Every now and again, one or other of them would trip on the stones and small rocks that littered the floor of the tunnel. Chetham would stumble into Atlanta, with Atlanta turning and helping him up; then a few moments later she would be on the floor and was being helped up by the strong hands of Chetham. It wasn't long before they started to find it funny.

'We're like two men who get so drunk they can't help each other keep upright,' giggled Atlanta.

'Well said there, young Henry. You have a way with words. It's good that we can laugh at our predicament. It's helping to keep more unpleasant thoughts at bay.'

'What thoughts are those, sire?'

'Why, that we may be betrayed.'

'How come?'

'The way may be blocked ahead of us, and the warden, knowing this, could then inform the soldiers, and they could pursue us down here and we would be trapped like rats. Or it could be worse, Henry: we could be forced to retrace our steps back to the well, and then find that no one responded to our cries for assistance. We would perish in this God-forsaken dark.'

Atlanta stopped and turned round to face Chetham.

'How can you say such a thing? Mr. Fielding and the warden, they're honourable men. They would not betray you!'

'Ah, lad, you speak with the voice of youth – you do not know how money can tempt a man.'

'But if you were to perish, the King wouldn't get his money, so what good would that be?'

'Oh, he would have my money – he would have his hands on the whole of my estate, for he could claim I was his debtor, and, having died owing him, my lands and my assets would be forfeit to the crown. Besides, I have no heirs.'

The words he spoke filled Atlanta with an icy fear. She turned round so that Chetham could not see her reach under her clothes and slip her hand into the space bag. She took out the phone: it was dead – the display page had no light – and when she pressed the black button there was nothing. No response at all. She stared at it in disbelief. It must mean, she thought, that being so far under the ground the signals from SHARP could not reach her. Now she began to panic. Could it be that she would never get out of the tunnel, never see daylight again? Never return to her mum, her home? The most dreadful thoughts crowded in on her.

She sat down, her back against the sharp rocks of

the tunnel wall, barely bothering to take the precaution of putting the phone back into the space bag. Paralysing, unreasoning fear had her in its grip again. Chetham stooped down and sat beside her. No longer the strong, confident merchant, he too was despairing. They sat without saying a word for several minutes. The air itself seemed to choke them. It was terrifying to imagine the candle in the lantern going out and the utter blackness that would surround them. Then a thought slipped quietly into Atlanta's mind, and she said it out loud:

'This is 1631.'

'It is indeed, the Lord's year sixteen hundred and thirty-one. I had thought to live a few years more.'

'And so you will.' Atlanta said, a huge smile spreading over her face. She shook his arm. 'Come on, we must not let fear defeat us.' Chetham lifted his head.

'What makes you so sure, lad?'

'God has more work for you.' Atlanta knew she must not tell him that she knew that the actual date of his death was 1653: that would make Henry Butterworth seem like a fortune teller – not a good thing to be. But by mentioning God she had in fact provided just the right encouragement.

'You speak well, Henry Butterworth – 'tis not becoming for a man of my education to lose heart in these trying circumstances.' They both scrambled to their feet, shaking off the dreadful thoughts that had overcome them.

They walked on, and soon came to the door that barred their way. Between the doorframe and the rock wall, exactly as the warden had described to them, was a small gap – a very small gap. Holding the lantern in front of her, Atlanta bent down and squeezed through to the other side.

Once through, she turned to look for the handle of the door, but then froze. There, curled up at the base of the door, was a huge snake. It was asleep, but the light from the lantern was beginning to disturb it. Atlanta choked back her feelings of horror at the creature.

'Sire,' she whispered, 'I need your cloak. Please could you pass it through the gap? As quickly as possible.'

Chetham didn't ask why, he just undid the ties of the fine woollen cloak at his shoulders and passed it through to her. Atlanta took it and, creeping near to the snake – which was luckily still dozy – opened the cloak wide and dropped it over the creature. Quickly she scooped together the edges, making a bundle that now contained a fat, and no doubt thoroughly confused, snake. There were some large pieces of rock strewn on the floor, and she used these to anchor the edges of the cloak while she quickly turned the handle of the door. Chetham pushed hard on it from the other side, so that it swung open with a rusty, grinding creak.

'What did you need my cloak for, Henry?' Chetham walked towards his cloak, puzzled by the large stones holding down the edges, and was just about to pick it up when Atlanta grabbed his hand.

'No, sire! There's a serpent under that cloak. It was asleep against the door. I used the cloak to secure it.'

Chetham drew his sword and gingerly flicked open the cloak, at which the snake, more afraid of them than they of it, slid away from them in the direction they had come.

'I'm so glad it decided to go back towards the well,' said Chetham. 'Hopefully we will not meet with others of its kind. We must be nearing the end of the tunnel by now.'

After the door, the ground seemed to go upwards, and before long they reached some stone steps.

At the top of the steps was an iron grill which Chetham, using all his strength, was able to slide to one side. Once up and out of the tunnel they found themselves in what must have been the crypt of the church. There were several stone sarcophaguses, and against one wall some more steps that led up to another grating. This time, however, a small amount of light filtered down. Gingerly Chetham slid back this second grating, and they both heaved themselves into the dimness of the church – some light filtered in through small and darkly coloured stained-glass windows, but they could see that they were quite alone.

'Now, lad, all that remains to be seen is whether Mr. Fielding managed to ensure that his horse was brought from the Sawyers Arms and tethered to the church post.'

'I'll go outside and see,' said Atlanta.

'No, wait a minute, lad. Answer me this: Am I correct in thinking that you will go to the grammar school at the warden's expense, but that you will have to work for this generous beneficence?'

'Aye, sire, that is what I hope will come about,' said Atlanta.

'And what will you do then?'

'I will hope to go into trade as you have done,

and so to prosper.'

'I had a vision in that tunnel,' said Chetham. 'There are many boys orphaned as you in the towns of Salford and Manchester, and if they are as brave and true as you, then trade and commerce has need of them. You will not pay for your tuition, my boy, for I shall, and clothed you shall be as well. When you are schooled and of age you must come to me again, if I should live. Seek me out, Henry, for I have plans for you. Now, if all this is to come to pass I shall need to escape the King. Go out and see if my horse is waiting.'

The horse was tethered to the church bridle post. Chetham mounted quickly, and not a moment too soon, because round the corner came the King's men. Chetham spurred his mount, and Atlanta watched as he galloped away. And as he went she could feel the mobile pulsing. She turned and went back into the church, and slipped into one of the boxed pews. She could hear someone entering the church – perhaps the Kings men to grab her. She quickly slipped out of the clothes, dialled 15799...and pressed the red button. She heard a far-off whining noise coming nearer and then...Nothing.

CHAPTER 10

Safe

Atlanta opened her eyes. She was back in her nana's bathroom. Returned safely to the twenty-first century and to exactly the same spot! She pulled on her jeans, wondering how long she had been gone, and then, before she had zipped them up, she heard the sound of the front door opening. Someone carried in heavy bags and put them down with a thump.

'That'll be four pounds thirty, missus.' The taxi driver's gruff voice could easily be heard upstairs, and then there was the sound of the front door shutting.

'Atlanta!' called her nana.

'I'm in the bathroom,' Atlanta called back in a quavering voice. She had suddenly started shaking uncontrollably. Shivers ran through her, overwhelming every part of her body. She sat down on the bathroom chair and hugged herself tightly, trying to stop the shakes. Must be some sort of delayed shock, she thought to herself.

A few minutes later her nana was tapping at the door.

'What's taking you so long, Atlanta? Other people need the toilet you know. Tesco was packed, and I had to wait ages for a taxi.' It was just like Nana Prestwich to refer to herself as 'other people', especially when it came to things like needing the toilet.

'Sorry, Nana, I...don't feel so well. I'll be out in a moment.' Atlanta flushed the toilet and quickly thrust her arms through her top. When she pulled it down, her fingers left smudgy, dirty marks. She looked down at her open palms and realised that they were covered in dusty grime: dirt from the tunnel! Dirt from 1631! The thought was unbelievable – it was so strange that it seemed to stop the shaking.

Quickly she turned the basin taps on, picked up the soap and worked up a thick lather. She could feel her nana's impatience through the door at the time she was taking to wash her hands.

'I know it's good to be thorough when you wash you hands, Atlanta, but there is reason in all things,' came through the door.

Atlanta hid her hands behind her back as she emerged from the bathroom, conscious that her fingernails were still clogged with dirt.

'Sit down on the sofa and I'll see what's up with you when I get down.' Nana Prestwich hardly gave Atlanta a glance, so great was her hurry to get into the bathroom and shut the door. A good thing, as Atlanta still had her hair tied back with the small piece of material that had been at the bottom of the bag she had opened on the banks of the River Irwell.

When Nana Prestwich got downstairs, she declared that Atlanta was feverish. After administering the dreaded Dr. Lacey's, she sent Atlanta home in a

taxi. 'Much too ill to go home on the bus,' she said to Martine, when she phoned to tell her that Atlanta was on her way in a taxi. 'She had that dreadful day-dreamy look of hers with knobs on,' she reported. 'And she told me that she felt sick – but I tell you what, there was nothing wrong with her appetite. Ate more than usual.' Every Saturday, when Nana Prestwich got back from Tesco, she heated up two pies, one for her and one for Atlanta. Atlanta usually just picked at hers, but stumbling through dark tunnels had made her incredibly hungry.

Atlanta was very glad to be in bed. At home in the familiar bedroom that she shared with Geneva she felt safe. And safe felt very nice. She was just beginning to take in the enormity of what had happened. Now, there were hundreds of questions she wanted to ask Mela. How had she done? Had she come up to expectations? Had the people at SHARP received any information? She also wanted to know: did SHARP lose contact when she was underground? She was obviously gone from the present day for much more than five or six minutes. Nana Prestwich had been out of the house for over two hours. In twenty-first century time she must have been away almost two hours. Her time in the past, from when she had landed on the river bank until she had watched Humphrey Chetham ride away, must have been about three, maybe four hours. Something didn't add up.

Atlanta waited impatiently through the next week for a contact message from SHARP. It came one week later. Having escaped a shopping trip by saying that she needed to practice her violin for the next Chetham interview, Atlanta was alone in the house. Mum, Geneva and Lincoln had gone out shopping. She had just finished playing the Bach piece she was planning to perform for Dr. Smallwood and his colleagues for the second time when she felt her phone vibrating. Pressing the green button, the vivid blue screen always used by SHARP hovered just a few feet away from the phone. As before, swirling colours spun off the screen, and then a message from Mela appeared.

Hello, Atlanta. I am sorry it has taken me a while to get back in touch with you. I know you will have been waiting anxiously for the results of your trip. The reason for the delay was that my work was checked extremely thoroughly before I was allowed to talk to you again. But everything is fine. Is it possible for you to go on your computer? I know it's switched off at the moment, but if you put it on I can send you messages, just the same as on your phone, but it means that you can type in anything you want to say to me.

Atlanta rushed upstairs to her bedroom and switched on the computer that she shared with Geneva. The same message that had been on her phone appeared on the screen, and at the bottom there was a button with the words 'post your reply' beside it. Atlanta quickly typed in: I've been so anxious wanting to know how I did.

You did brilliantly – absolutely brilliantly. Everyone was amazed that you were so good; I think they thought that you might be too scared or perhaps too sensitive to be a good time traveller. We know you were scared at times, but you conquered your fears. Did you enjoy the experience?

Atlanta read the words a few times and then typed in: I did enjoy it, I really can't explain why, but it was amazing. Are you sure I did OK?

It was so important for Atlanta to know from her new friend that she had been successful.

You certainly did, Atlanta. I was proved absolutely right in choosing you as a time traveller, though many doubted it. The only trouble was, we lost contact with you when you went down the tunnel. SHARP didn't realise that at the depth you were and with the particular configuration of the tunnel we would lose contact. There was some discussion over whether I had been at fault. We saw you going down the well, and then nothing until you came out into the church.

Why would they think it was your fault?

It was mostly because there had been a terrible to-do about losing Danny Higgins on his third journey. SHARP nearly lost him – he could have been stuck forever in the time known as the Dark Ages.

That sounds really scary. What caused it?

It was not a SHARP malfunction, believe me. It was stupidity on the part of the operator.

Was that the boy you were telling me about? The one that was supposed to be so good?

No, it wasn't Kaz. He was exonerated completely and actually played an important part in the rescue. No it was a girl – what a blow for us girls.

Was the twenty-first century boy alright? Did you say his name is Danny Higgins?

Yes, he was fine once he got back. His name is Danny Higgins and I am telling you that because SHARP have decided that it would be a good idea for you two to communicate. Would that be alright with you, Atlanta?

I don't see why not, but how would we communicate?

Are you familiar with any of the social networking sites of your time?

My mum doesn't let me go on anything like Facebook.

I can understand that, but Danny has set up a blog of his own, retelling his adventures back in time. Everyone thinks they are just imaginative stories, and he is getting quite a following. He invites kids to send in their own stories of time travel adventures, and quite a few have. The stories are lots of fun, loads of brilliant ideas. You could ask your mum if you could upload a story. You could write the one about meeting Humphrey Chetham and your adventure in the tunnel.

Oh, that would be great. I'd really like to do that. But if I send it to him, he will just think it is another kid with a made-up story.

Yes, but you will include a sentence or maybe a word that we have given you that will tell Danny your story is for real. I've got to go soon, Atlanta. Do you have any questions?

Will I be able to go back in time again?

Oh yes, we will be in touch with you again, very soon. There is a very special journey that SHARP want you to take. They know that you, and only you, are the right person for this project.

Atlanta's eyes widened when she read this, and she sat back on the sofa with a bump. What could it be? Mela had told her so many amazing things that her head was spinning, but Mela hadn't logged off yet.

Now I've just one request.

What is it, Mela?

I would love to hear you play. Could you leave your computer on and just play me one piece?

Of course I could. I'll get my violin – it's downstairs. Atlanta hurtled down the stairs and back up again, clutching her violin and bow.

When she got back the message on the screen said:

I would love to hear you play the carol 'Silent Night.'

Atlanta looked at it, puzzled. Then she thought that perhaps it was Christmas in Mela's time. The previous Christmas, Atlanta had worked on a variation on the theme of Silent Night, but she had been disappointed with it and had never played it to anyone. Now she started playing, standing in front of the computer, for Mela, and as she did, wonderful melodic variations came into her head. Almost in a trance she played and played, and the music became more and more beautiful.

When she put the violin down she saw the words on the screen:

Beautiful music always crosses the time barrier –

thank you, Atlanta, and goodbye...Mela.

Atlanta wanted to type in: but you were playing as well. She had no doubt at all that Mela, in her future time zone, had been playing her violin at the same time – she had heard it in her head.

Just then there was a pounding of feet on the stairs and Geneva came in holding two carrier bags. 'Mum's got me the most fantastic pair of jeans and this top; it's so cool. Oh, and she bought you a new top to wear when you go for your second interview at Chets' (Atlanta still referred to the music school by its full name, but cool dude Geneva used the name all the students gave it).

CHAPTER 11

One Shilling and Tuppence

A week later, Atlanta went to stay at Simon's for the weekend. Simon's house seemed huge to Atlanta. It had three storeys. His room, where he could practice on his own, was large enough for a piano, several music stands and a comfy sofa. Although they lived in a big house, Simon's parents didn't have a lot of money, but what they had they spent on Simon. His dad was a poet, and occasionally sold small books of poetry; his mother painted and occasionally sold her pictures of dark, scary landscapes. They loved Atlanta, and they were always asking her to stay. They had been friends of Martine's from way back.

The weekend had been fine, one of the first nice days of spring. They had all gone for a walk at Sale Water Park and Simon and Atlanta had had fun chasing around after a ball, like all the other kids, but when they got home, unlike other kids, they spent the evening in Simon's music room. Atlanta played him her variations on 'Silent Night.'

'That's amazing, Atlanta,' said Simon when she

had finished. 'It's just amazing.'

'Do you think it's good enough to play for the people at Chetham's?'

'Of course it is, Atlanta. You know, you are going to be famous – a famous violinist. You'll be a star!'

'You'll be a great violinist as well, Simon.'

'Oh no! Definitely not. I'm not going to go on doing music, you know.'

'What? Your mum and dad will be so disappointed.'

'Maybe. But I'm the sensible one in the family. Those two – don't get me wrong, I love them – have just got their heads in the clouds. You know this house, it's practically falling down. Look up there.' Simon pointed to a grey patch on the ceiling in one corner of the room. 'That damp patch is from water coming in. The roof's got loads of holes and there's no way they can afford to get it repaired.'

'But your dad's lovely books – people buy them. He's a famous poet.'

Simon shook his head.

'You don't make any money from poetry books; well, not much. No, I'm going to be a banker and make loads of dosh. Someone in this family has to make money, and I reckon it's got to be me.'

'But won't you miss playing?'

'I can still play the violin in my spare time. I shall be a 'talented amateur,' and you will be famous, and I'll be able to buy tickets to the concert hall where you are playing and come and sit in the front row.'

Atlanta always stayed in the same room when she stayed with Simon. Now, as she was getting ready for bed, she looked round and realised that the room was shabby, very shabby. The wallpaper was faded, the paint round the windowsill was peeling and there were loads of damp patches on the ceiling. Whenever Atlanta was planning a visit to Simon's, Geneva always shuddered and said: 'I don't know how you can sleep in that spooky old house with those dreadful carpets and curtains.' Geneva noticed stuff like carpets and curtains; Atlanta never did. She looked down at the carpet and realised it was very threadbare.

She snuggled down in bed and had started to drift off to sleep when her phone began to vibrate with the strange pulse that she now recognised as SHARP getting in touch. She sat up in bed and pressed the black button. The screen did not slide away as before. Instead there was a text message:

Hello, Atlanta, we have the instructions for your second trip back in time, but we know that you are at your friend's house. Will you be disturbed? Mela

She sent a text message back: Maybe, sometimes Simon's mum comes up to say goodnight.

We will wait, then, until later tonight.

Atlanta lay in bed listening to the old clock on the landing chiming the hour. She got drowsy around ten o'clock and must have fallen asleep because she was woken by the vibration from her mobile, and just then the clock chimed twelve. She sat up, wide-awake. She pressed the black button and the following text message appeared.

Hello again – are you ready to go?

Atlanta sent back a one word text: Yes.

Then the screen enlarged and slid away from the mobile to hover a few feet in front of her.

‹Time Zone›
23rd December 1940

‹Place›

The City of Manchester

‹Landing›

A row of shops on a street behind the cathedral

‹Instructions›

Find the sweet shop, look for the key under the plant pot in the window box. Let yourself in and go up the stairs at the back of the shop. In one of the bedrooms you will find some girl's clothes. Get dressed and take the musical instrument that you find there with you.

‹Destination›

The cathedral. It is only a few streets away. You will need to go down into the air raid shelters under the cathedral.

‹Conditions›

Very dangerous. We are protecting you with a shield. Don't be alarmed, you cannot be hurt, but you will see devastation and destruction. Our presence throughout your participation will protect those that need protecting, and we can limit the damage to the cathedral.

‹Equipment›
Mobile phone, travel bag. Mobile phone fitted with beam of light activated when t-o-r-c-h is keyed in (only use sparingly).

If you wish to travel, do as follows:

› take off your clothes; put on your swimming costume
› press the time/space travel bag close to your body so that it is attached; key in 15799
› press the green button

We will be with you all the way on this trip – it is a great service you are doing at a time when many were serving the good of all.

As she had done last time, Atlanta paid close attention to the instructions. This time, though, when she looked at the date she couldn't believe it: she was travelling back to Manchester at the time of the Second World War. World War TWO! That was incredible! They had done so much about the war when she was in Mrs. Grant's class in Year 5. She had been captivated by the book they had read: 'Good Night Mister Tom', and she had loved writing about being an evacuee. She remembered the time when the old and very this particular house. It must have been number ten because next to it, still standing, but with missing windows and a front door askew, was number twelve.

All the excitement that she had felt a few minutes earlier drained away as the reality of where she had arrived sank in. She half ran, half hobbled as best she could in her bare feet to the other side of the street where there was a row of shops. Luckily, there were no broken bricks on this side. With shaking hands, she opened the time/space travel bag that was still firmly in place on her tummy and took out the silver disc, pressed it to her forehead and felt the backing slip away into her fingers. She put it into the bag, slipping the mobile in as well, and snapped the bag shut. Then she examined the first shop. It had two long windows protected by wooden shutters, which offered no clue as to what it sold. But from the light of the flames coming from the fires now burning in the city she could just make out the shop sign: 'Macintyre's Gunsmiths Est 1892' – obviously not a sweet shop. She walked quickly on up the street. Her feet were numb and she was beginning to shiver uncontrollably. She passed a pet shop and two bookshops, and then came to one that had a few jars of sweets and a couple of boxes advertising toffee bars in the window. At the back of the in the middle of the small shop stood a big wooden counter with a glass front. Through it Atlanta could see an untidy stack of boxes. She peered closely and could see that they were full of sherbet fountains and strings of liquorice. On the top of the counter stood some brass scales with little weights lined up neatly in a row, but what really caught Atlanta's eye was the till, which was sitting in pride of place on the counter. It was huge, made of some kind of metal, with a fancy ornate pattern all over the sides. It was the same shape as the plastic tills that she remembered in the play shop at nursery school, but much larger. She could see that the last amount to be rung up was 1s and 2d.

Suddenly, fascinated by this ancient accounting machine, Atlanta nipped round the other side of the counter where the shopkeeper would have stood. She pressed down two of the large round keys. The till made a pinging sound and the money drawer shot open. At the top, the sum of 3s and 6d was now displayed. Forgetting her fear of exploding bombs and being frozen to death, not too mention any thoughts of intruding on other people's property, Atlanta peered into the money drawer. It was empty except for one large round brown coin and two smaller ones, also brown. She took them out and examined them under the torchlight. They were one penny and two half-penny coins. Carefully placing them back in the drawer, she pushed it shut and then couldn't resist having another go, pinging up 1s and 2d to return the display to its original amount.

She turned away from the counter and swept a beam of light around the shop. To Atlanta it looked very shabby and dull compared to present-day shops, but according to the times, this shop was doing well. Small wooden shelving behind the counter held packets of cigarettes with brand names she didn't recognise, like Wills Woodbines and Senior Service. To one side there were rows and rows of jars filled with a huge assortment of sweets. Fascinated, Atlanta went close to peer at the labels. There were fizz bombs, sherbet lemons, peppermint creams, jelly beans, fruit gums and liquorice comfits. She stared in amazement at the colours.

CHAPTER 12

Susan's Violin

At the back of the shop a curtained doorway separated the shop from the house were the family lived. The stairs must be through there, she thought. Now the cold was beginning to really hurt. She must find some clothes quickly! She went through the doorway and up the stairs. At the top there was a small landing with three doors leading off. The first door she tried had a large bed in it, a massive wardrobe and a chest of drawers. At the bottom of the bed was a toddler's cot. Atlanta peered around, but there were no clothes.

The next bedroom was much smaller and, with relief, she saw that there was a pile of clothes on the bed. On the top was a pair of grey woollen socks. She sat down and dragged the socks on to her frozen feet. They came up to her knees. Next on the pile was a thick white vest made out some sort of material that felt slightly furry to the touch. Almost as soon as she had it on, she began to feel warmer. There were some large navy-blue knickers that she didn't bother with, because of the swimming costume. Then there was a blue-flowered cotton dress, followed by a thick grey woollen jumper, and finally a grey coat that reached down to below her knees and buckled at the waist. Tucked in neatly on the floor beside the clothes was a pair of brown lace-up shoes. Fully dressed, Atlanta sat down on the bed and could feel warmth beginning to circulate round her body. Old-fashioned clothes seemed warmer than those worn in modern times. Then she spotted what looked like a note on the little bedside table. She reached over and read it:

> Dear Susan,
> If you are reading this I know it will be about 5 o'clock, and you will have come back home from Grandad's. I do hope you haven't, because they say the bombing is going to be bad tonight, and it will be much safer for you in Denton with Grandad. I know how much you love your violin, but even if it is a stradiwhatsit, it's not worth risking your life for. If you have come back, put on the clothes I've left on the bed for you. They're warmer than your school ones, and what you must do is go straight to the cathedral air-raid shelter. As you know, Mr. and Mrs.

McIntyre have kindly offered to take me and baby to their house in Sale while this bombing is bad.

Love

Mother

As soon as she read the note, Atlanta wondered what time it was. She jumped up and ran down the stairs, remembering that she had heard the ticking of a clock. A sweep with the beam of the torch around the shop walls picked out a large round clock high up above the door. It showed the time in roman numerals: one fifteen. It was the middle of the night, and it was obvious that Susan had been sensible and stayed in Denton.

Back in Susan's room, Atlanta looked around for the violin. She couldn't see it anywhere. Then she read the note again: 'stradiwhatsit?' she murmured out loud. Could it possibly be a Stradivarius? Surely not, but if it were, it would probably be kept out of sight. She looked at the long candlewick counterpane that hung down over the bed to the floor. On hands and knees she lifted it up and peered under the bed. She could just see a long wooden box. She pulled it out. Although it had a latch with a padlock in it, the padlock wasn't closed properly. She opened it up and there was a violin case. Trembling with excitement, Atlanta lifted it out and put it down on the bed. She opened the case. On the dark blue satin lining on the inside of the case there was a label with the word 'Stradivarius' embroidered in gold. Atlanta was staring at a genuine Stradivarius violin!

'Oh my goodness, I can't believe it! I'm looking at a Strad!' The words seemed to hang in the cold air of the little bedroom. Outside, the rumble of destruction was an insignificant background noise to this unbelievable moment in Atlanta's life.

As Atlanta locked the door of the shop and replaced the key under the plant pot, she held the precious violin case tightly in her hand. Conscious now of the danger around her from the furious glow of fires out of control in the city centre, she was anxious to get to the safety of the cathedral. But when she got to the bottom of the street she stopped for a moment, turned and looked back up towards the shop. As she did so, a tremendous noise filled her ears. A bomb exploded on the very spot where only a few moments before she had been standing. Ken and May Hardy's Sweets and Cigarette shop took a direct hit. The walls collapsed into a heap of rubble and a cloud of dust bloomed up

CHAPTER 13

The Air Raid Shelter

Atlanta sat with her elbows on her knees and her hands covering her ears, trying to blot out the dreadful sounds around her. 'I can't do this,' she thought, the tears trickling down her face. 'I just can't do this… I want to go home.' She had slipped the mobile into the pocket of Susan's best coat and she was fingering the buttons, thinking of getting it out and pressing the emergency button. But even as those thoughts went through her head, she knew that she couldn't just leave the precious violin there on the pavement.

As she stared at the slabs of paving stones, she became aware that a pair of sturdy black boots, covered in dust and grime, had stopped in front of her.

'Not lost are you, luv?' came a voice from above the boots. Atlanta's eyes tracked upwards past a very dirty blue uniform to an equally grimy face underneath a metal hat with a wide brim. She could just make out the initials ARP on the front. She had learnt what that meant in school.

Atlanta, wiped a sleeve across the tears on her

face.

'Are you Air Raid Precautions?' she asked.

'That's right, dear, Come on, we'll soon get you somewhere safe. You're right near the cathedral shelter, you know.' The man bent forward and put a hand under Altanta's arm.

'I didn't know which way to go there,' said Atlanta, as if to explain why she was crying. The three streets in front of her went in different directions, but that wasn't the reason for her tears.

'Now they've removed the street names, anyone can get lost, but all you need do is to take this little street here, and when it comes out on to the big road – that's Cross Street – turn right and you'll see the cathedral in front of you. But go quick. Once those devils up in the sky get a fix on Victoria Station they'll be dropping bombs like fury round here. The trouble is, the flames are lighting the place up for them. They say they knew how to find Manchester by heading towards the glow from Liverpool – bombed that to bits last night, they did.'

'Oh, no!' exclaimed Atlanta, feeling as if she was going to cry again.

'Not got relatives there, have you?'

'No, no…it's just that it's all so horrid.'

'I know, miss, but go quickly now. Err...what's that you've got with you?'

'My violin.'

'Mind if I take a look? I know it sounds daft, but you could be a German spy with a radio or summat in there, and I should be checking.' Atlanta opened the violin case. The man smiled and indicated to her to shut it up again.

'Get along now as quick as you can – I'd come with you but I can't, I've got to get up to Piccadilly – they need all the help they can get up there.' Atlanta looked into the tired, drawn face of the ARP warden and suddenly realised how brave he was, doing his duty on this terrible night.

'Thank you very much. I'll be fine again now,' she said. 'You've given me the courage I needed.' He patted her shoulder, gave her wave and was off into the night.

Just as he had said, the small street led down on to a wide open road, and when she turned and looked along it to the right, Altanta could see the outline of Manchester Cathedral, less than a five minute walk away.

Here on this main thoroughfare into Manchester from Salford there were many more people. Most of them were in a uniform of some sort, like the ARP man. Up the street to the right, a double-decker bus had been blown up. It was lying in the road, upside down, the front tipped into the crater made by the bomb, its back wheels sticking up incongruously into the night air. Surely anyone who had been on that bus would not have survived?

As she walked towards the cathedral, Atlanta was amazed to see horse-drawn carts going by. The blinkered horses, with barrels of water or piles of sand-bags in their carts, clattered along at a brisk pace, swerving to miss obstacles like the upturned bus. Further on to the left, down Deansgate, she could just see firemen holding hoses, attacking a blaze that had got hold of a complete building, all of it outlined in a fiery red against the night sky.

Up in the sky, two bright beams of light were criss-crossing the blackness. She could see a plane caught in the light of the beams; then a noise she hadn't heard before: the rapid fire of anti-aircraft guns. Puffs of smoke from exploding shells dotted here and there around the plane, but it didn't go down, it flew on and disappeared into the night sky, out of the range of the guns.

When Atlanta reached the cathedral she started

to go up the steps. But then someone pulled at her arm.

'Where are you going, kid?' Atlanta turned and looked into the face of a young woman. She was wearing a grey overcoat. A felt hat with a badge on the front with the letters AFS held down her bouncy, blonde curls.

'I thought there was an air raid shelter under the cathedral,' said Atlanta.

'There is, but you don't get to it that way. Follow me.' She led the way across the street to an opening in the wall. They went down a steep flight of stairs and turned a corner, and in the darkness Atlanta could just make out another flight, leading further down.

'We're right near to the river here. Years ago these steps used to lead down to a landing stage, and people would board pleasure boats to take them on trips up the canal – imagine that!'

At the bottom, a steel door was guarded by an old-looking chap. He wore a steel helmet, had a grey moustache and carried a rifle. A strange flat bag with a red cross on it was strapped to his chest.

'In you go me lovelies,' he said, winking at the young woman with Atlanta.

They pushed through the doors. On the other side was a long tunnel. Then they came to a room where people were lying on rows of bunk beds. Children were sleeping, two or three to a bunk. Some women were also asleep, but a few were sitting knitting or chatting quietly.

'Are you tired?' asked the young woman. 'I could see if I could find some space for you.' She nodded towards the bunks.

'Not really,' replied Atlanta.

'What on earth were you doing wandering about so late at night, and tonight of all nights? I thought everyone had heard that there was going to be a raid tonight. And what's your name by the way?'

'I'm Susan '

'Susan what?'

'Susan Hardy,' lied Atlanta.

'Well, Susan, my name's Dorothy.' They shook hands in a formal way and then smiled at each other. Dorothy was very pretty.

'And what are you doing out on your own?'

'Well, I was at my grandad's in Denton and I wanted to go home. I got a bus most of the way but then I had to walk – we live in the city centre you see. I didn't realise there would be a problem. My mum had told me to stay at grandad's, but I wanted to go home and get my violin.' Atlanta found herself recounting what could have been Susan's life without any difficulty, as if it were her own.

'A bit daft, wasn't it?'

'Yes, you're right, it was a bit daft,' said Atlanta, thinking that what was a bit daft was her accepting SHARP's invitation to travel back to Manchester in the middle of a bombing raid.

'Well, I can't talk. It was my night off. I'm in the Auxiliary Fire Service; I should be on the phones, but I had worked non-stop for a month, so I'm not going to feel guilty. Anyway, I said I would meet my boyfriend off the train – he's in the army but he hasn't shown up; good job, really. I think the train must have been held up somewhere on the way – I hope he's somewhere safer than Manchester tonight. Come on, we'll go and see if there is anything we can do to help. I've been down here before and the WRVS are always short-handed.'

'WRVS – who are they?' asked Atlanta, thinking that during World War Two there was a bewildering number of different services all identified by their initial letters.

'Don't you know? It's the Women's Royal Voluntary Service, all the ancient old biddies like my mum have joined up to that – they dish out tea and sandwiches, if they've got any.'

Atlanta giggled: 'You're not being very respectful, are you?'

'You've got to laugh at life, kid, or you'd be a gonna – that's what I like about Sammy, my boyfriend, he's always telling jokes.'

'Do you miss him?'

'All the time, but…' Dorothy shrugged, 'you just get on and do the best you can.'

The next room was crowded with people, mainly men in uniform, sitting on long benches at wooden canteen tables. Those who couldn't find a place on a bench sat on the floor on blankets. To one side there was a long trestle table with huge tea urns steaming gently. One grey-haired woman (definitely one of Dorothy's 'old biddies,' thought Atlanta) was pouring milk from a large jug into a long line of metal cups. Obviously the reason why this room was so crowded was that people were hoping for a cup of tea.

Dorothy went up to her and introduced herself and her companion, 'Susan.' The woman said her name was Joan and that she was rushed off her feet.

'Do you need any help?' Dorothy asked.

'Now what does it look like, luv? Ethel was supposed to be down 'ere with me tonight, but I think she's got trapped t'other side of town – she lives in Longsight, so she'll not be getting across now. Bert says there's fires up at Piccadilly and down Market Street.'

All the while Joan was speaking she was pouring the milk into the many waiting tin cups. 'The blokes over there have just come in – they've been travelling all day. There's been no chance of them being billeted anywhere yet – they're from Poland, so the officer in charge says. Fliers they are, by their uniforms. Anyway. If you can get the trays out from under the table and take the cups of tea to them and give 'em one of those slices of bread and marg,' she nodded her head towards a gigantic pile of sliced bread teetering at the end of the table, 'it will be a big help, cos then they won't have to line up – that causes mayhem. One slice only, mind you.'

'Rightie-ho Joan, we'll do our best, won't we, Susan?' Dorothy fished out the huge trays from under the table.

'Yes, of course,' said Atlanta. She put the precious violin down near a protective wall and grabbed the tray that Dorothy was holding out to her.

Joan now picked up the massive aluminium teapot and started pouring the hot brown liquid into the cups. First Dorothy filled her tray with cups and then helped Atlanta to put some on her tray, although not as many as on her own, judging she was too little to carry a full load. They counted out the appropriate number of slices of bread and marg, and Joan put a bowl of sugar and a teaspoon on each tray. She ordered them to ask people how many sugars they wanted. Dorothy set off quickly with a bright smile on her face.

'Now then, Susan, slow but sure – we don't want the tea spilt do we? And remember: only one slice each,' Joan said, as Atlanta, holding her massive tray as firmly as she could, sallied forth towards a table of young men. As she approached, they all grinned broadly at her. She put the tray down on the table and started handing the cups round, asking each young man in turn whether they wanted sugar.

They all said 'thank you' in a strong foreign accent and showed how many sugars by raising one, two or three fingers. It was obvious that most spoke very little English. But one man did; he was quite fluent, though with a strong accent.

'You have saved our lives, miss. We were dying of thirst.'

'Have you come far today?'

'Yes, we were billeted near the south coast, but they sent us up here; the train was very slow and kept stopping. We are pilots, and we are going to fly for the British Air Force. We will fly their Hurricanes. We will continue the struggle against the invaders of our homeland from here in England. They beat us in Poland, and many of our compatriots died; we are the ones that escaped, and we will continue the struggle until the death.' The man looked very serious as he spoke.

'That's very brave of you,' Atlanta said. 'Your country will be proud of you when the war is over.'

'Thank you, young lady; that is a kind thing to say.' He translated Atlanta's words into Polish for his companions. They smiled at Atlanta, and then they all stood up and gave her a small, old-fashioned bow.

Atlanta went back to Joan, who filled her tray with another round of cups and slices of bread. Atlanta could see Dorothy half way down the hall by now: she was much quicker and more efficient than she was at dispensing the hot mugs to the waiting hands and swizzling in the required number of spoonfuls of sugar. After about half an hour, it seemed that everyone had been served. Joan said that if anyone wanted a second cup, they could come to the urn and get it

CHAPTER 14

Silent Night

Atlanta put the violin case carefully on the table in front of her. She hadn't wanted tea, but Dorothy sat with her hands round a cup, sipping the warm liquid and watching her young friend.

Atlanta opened the case up. She picked up the violin and looked at it, turning it over. Near the left-hand shoulder she noticed a small scratch. She peered at it carefully and rubbed it with her forefinger. Without a doubt it was a faint but recognisable 's.' Had Susan scratched the initial of her first name on to this valuable violin? Or had someone done it to identify it as a Stradivarius? In the small compartment at the end of the case there was a block of resin to rub on the bow and a card that said in round childish writing:

If this violin should go astray, please return it to Susan Hardy, The Sweet and Cigarette Shop, Shude Hill, Manchester.

Just then, a man with a flat cap and a somewhat desperate look on his face, who had just arrived from the outside, came and sat down at their table.

'You can get yourself some tea, you know,' Dorothy told him.

'Oh I'm too upset for tea, young lady,' he replied.

'Why what's the matter? Has your home been hit?'

'No, worse – the bastards (excuse my language)' he looked at them both, suddenly ashamed to be using words like that in front of two girls, 'they've... they've bombed the cathedral, that's what they've done!'

'Oh no!' exclaimed Dorothy and Atlanta in unison.

'They've taken out the regimental chapel, that's for sure – it's just a heap of rubble, and the glass windows are gone. Everywhere's a mess inside – the statue of the founder – I saw it lying on the floor.'

'You didn't go in, did you? said Dorothy, in a shocked voice. 'You shouldn't have done that – you should have gone down a shelter.'

'How could I?' The man shook his head from side to side. 'How could I?' he repeated. 'You see, the governor's left me in charge of the school, and the school means the cathedral an'all, don't it? Before he left, the governor said, 'Now, Dalton, you keep the place in good shape, we want it spick and span when we come back.' He left with the boys, you see – they've been evacuated to North Wales.'

'It's the hospital school you're talking about, isn't it?' asked Dorothy.

'Yes, miss, it is: the one that's been educating boys since its founder Sir Humphrey Chetham provided for it in 'is will.'

Atlanta had been looking closely at the man ever since he had started speaking, but when he had mentioned his name she had given a start.

'Are you Mr. Dalton?' she asked politely. He nodded. 'Do you have a wife and any children, Mr. Dalton?'

'Oh Aye. The missus, she's gone with the schoolboys and the governor to Wales. Safe as houses they'll be. But me lads now,' Dalton paused and his hand went to the inside pocket of his jacket, and his shoulders went back as a proud smile spread across his face, 'they're serving in His Majesty's Royal Navy, out on the high seas, facing goodness knows what danger.' He passed them two black and white photos of two young naval ratings in uniform, so similar in features it would be hard to tell it wasn't a photo of the same lad, except that one was smiling and one was serious.

'They're very alike,' said Dorothy.

'Oh aye, us Dalton's all look alike. This one here

smiling is our John, Jolly John we call him – always the life and soul of the party – and his brother is serious Samuel. Me missus says we must 'ave known what they would be like when we chose their names when they were born. And my name's Arthur, and everyone says that's 'ardworking Arthur.'

Atlanta was stunned for a moment as she realised that Arthur Dalton, the porter who had escorted her and her mum from the gate to meet Dr Smallwood, must be the son, no, the grandson, of this Arthur Dalton. The likeness was incredible.

Dorothy got up. 'I don't care what you say, Arthur. I think you should have a cup of tea.' She went over to Joan at the tea urn. She was gone a few minutes, Joan keeping her there for the comfort of a friendly chat.

'Now, miss, what's that you've got there?' Arthur Dalton nodded towards the violin.

'My violin,' replied Atlanta, blushing a little at the lie.

'Well, can you play it? I mean reasonable like, so people can recognise a tune?'

'Yes, I can.'

'Well, I suggest you get it out of the case and cheer everyone up with a bit of music. After all, you know, it's Christmas Eve now, even if those,' he paused, searching for a word that he might use in front of a young lady, 'b...German bombers up in the sky above our city don't,' he finished lamely.

'I don't know if people would like it. It might interrupt their conversations.'

'They will – anything to take their minds off things,' said Arthur Dalton.

Dorothy had come back with the tea and heard part of the conversation.

'Arthur's right, Susan, if you can play it would cheer everyone up. Perhaps a carol?

'Well, yes, of course, if you think people would enjoy it, I could play some carols.'

'I'm sure they would,' said Dorothy, leading Atlanta out into a small space in the centre of the room. As Atlanta put the instrument under her chin and lifted the bow, faces turned towards her and the chatter of talk died down. She thought for a moment and then started on the opening bars of 'While Shepherds Watch Their Flocks by Night.' The sound was true and clear. Atlanta was, after all, playing a Stradivarius. By the time she was into the second verse, people were singing; most knew the words but some just hummed. She came to the end, paused a second and then started on 'Once in Royal David's City', followed by ' Hark the Herald Angels Sing' and 'O Come, All Ye Faithful.' When she put her bow down there was clapping and shouts of 'encore, encore.'

The Polish flier who spoke good English got up and came over to her, another Polish man following him.

'You are a marvellous violinist, young lady. I never thought to hear such playing in this country and from one so young.'

'Thank you.' Atlanta blushed.

'Bernard here has a wonderful voice. He would like to sing with you, would that be alright?'

'Of course,' Atlanta replied. 'What would you like me to play?' she asked the one called Bernard. He was a young chap with a mop of curly brown hair and smiling eyes. He gave a big grin and spread out his hands to show that he couldn't speak a word of English. The other man translated what Atlanta had asked, and there were several exchanges in Polish before nods of the head and the first man said, 'He asks if you can play 'Silent Night.' It is a very special carol for us. We always sing it in our homes at Christmas.'

Atlanta didn't say anything for a minute. A strange, strange feeling came over as she remembered

Mela asking her to play this piece.

'Do you not know this Christmas song?'

'Oh yes, I know it very well.' Atlanta started playing a few bars of the variation she had played for Mela, and then she took the tune into the opening bars of one of the best-known carols in the world.

The young man started singing; the words were in Polish. He truly did have a wonderful voice. The audience was transfixed. One, two, three times they went through the carol, and when they stopped there was utter silence – then people stood up and stamped their feet and clapped and cheered. Dorothy came over and hugged Atlanta.

'What a wonderful musician! You darling girl!'

Just then Atlanta felt her phone starting to vibrate. She turned to the Polish man and said, 'Thank you for singing with me; you have a beautiful voice.'

He didn't understand a word she was saying but bowed to her, clapped his hands above his head, and then took hold of her hand and kissed it. He waved to the flier who spoke English, who jumped up and came over to them. The singer gabbled something in Polish to him.

'He wants to say to you that he will never forget you,' he told Atlanta.

'Please tell him I will never forget him,' Atlanta said, feeling her eyes fill with tears, knowing that the singer would be an old man or dead by the time she was born.

'I need to go to the toilet now,' she whispered to Dorothy, 'and I'm really tired – I'm going to go and find some room on a bunk to go to sleep.'

'You do that, darling.' Dorothy gave her another hug and kissed her lightly on the cheek.

'Oh, and would you look after my violin for me?'

'Of course I will. I'm not going to bed myself. I'll give Joan a hand with the clearing up. Good night – sweet dreams.'

Atlanta hurried towards the toilets, tears streaming down her face.

Inside the dimly lit toilet she took out her mobile. There was a text message from SHARP:

> Atlanta – we need you to go up out of the shelter as quickly as you can. We'll have difficulty transporting you back to the twenty-first century at the depth you are now. You are not so far down as on your first trip – we've still got contact but we need you out – NOW.

Brushing away her tears with the sleeve of

Susan's coat, Atlanta rushed up the steps, pushed open the heavy metal door and surprised the old chap on guard. He called out: 'Hey, where are you going young lady? The All Clear hasn't sounded yet.'

She streaked past up the stone steps to the road.

Almost out of breath, Atlanta paused and looked up and down the road – Where could she take off the clothes? Close to the cathedral, a small shop with its front window blown out had a door hanging on its hinges. Atlanta stepped inside, crunching on broken glass. She made her way to the back of the shop and crouched down behind the tall counter. Her hands were trembling and the tears were coming again, but she managed to put the clothes in a neat pile, dial 15799 and press the red button. She heard the far distant whine coming nearer and nearer, then… Nothing.

Two weeks after Atlanta had stayed at Simon's, a letter arrived at her house to inform Martine that Atlanta definitely had a place at Chetham's School of Music to start in September. There was also an invitation for Atlanta to come and play either the piano or the violin at the end of term concert, and the family were invited to attend. Atlanta told her mother that she would play the violin.

On the day of the concert, Nana Prestwich came down to look after Geneva and Lincoln. Martine had decided that they would probably get bored sitting through a concert of classical music, however good. Martine and Atlanta set off, just as they had on the day of the interview on the bus into Manchester, Atlanta's shabby violin wedged tightly between them.

When they arrived at the school, Dr. Smallwood's secretary came to meet them. She escorted Martine to the concert hall and then told Atlanta to follow her. She led Atlanta to a room set aside for those students who were going to perform. As she opened the door a hubbub of noise bubbled out. Atlanta joined a room full of noisy and exuberant students who looked about twice her size! They were all laughing and joking with each other, playing little snippets of tunes or talking animatedly on mobile phones. Atlanta sat on a bench. No one spoke to her, but she didn't mind because, of course, they didn't know her. What she did mind was getting her violin out. It looked so shabby in comparison to the quality of the other students' instruments. How could she play this battered old violin in front of a concert hall full of people! She saw a slim, attractive girl glance at it contemptuously. A teacher came in and rapped on a table.

'Quiet now, please! Can we have the Year 11 quartet? You know you are first on.'

Four students got up and left. The room was silent now except for the occasional hushed whisper, reprimanded by a frown from the teacher. Slowly the room emptied as groups or individuals got up with their instruments to play. As they left, Atlanta felt more and more dreadful. Her palms started to sweat; her throat became dry; she felt as scared as she had done when faced with the black hole of the well in 1631. And just as she had done then, she thought of running away. This time she didn't need to worry about ruining someone else's life. No one would notice if she didn't play – it wasn't life or death. She closed her violin case, went to the door and went out, bumping straight into Dr. Smallwood.

'Ah, Atlanta! I've come to take you on the stage myself.' He held her hand and led her back into the room and out through the other door into the concert hall. There was polite clapping as she came on. Dr. Smallwood adjusted the music stand and Atlanta stood beside him, petrified.

'This, ladies and gentlemen, is Atlanta Tully. She is to join us as a student next term. She is playing for you this afternoon because I would like you to hear why I am not sure at all what it is she will learn from us at Chet's.' He paused while there was some more polite clapping.

'I am going to ask her to play the violin that I have in this case. Many of you will know that it is the college's Stradivarius, acquired in 1955 by one of our staff whose eagle eye spotted it in a junk shop on Shude Hill. Such amazing finds could be made in those far-off days.'

Atlanta couldn't believe what she was hearing. As Dr. Smallwood passed her the instrument she looked down and saw, on the shoulder of the violin, a small but unmistakable 's.' She stared at the mark and then gently rubbed her finger on the wood, all the fear draining out of her mind and body.

'And what are you going to play for us, Atlanta?'

She didn't answer, but put the violin to her chin and played her own, musically wonderful variation on the theme of 'Silent Night.'

When she took the bow from her chin, there was silence for what seemed like an age, and then the hall erupted with clapping and cheering.

WATCH OUT FOR THE NEXT BOOKS IN THE EXCITING TIME TRAVELLER KIDS SERIES

Next in the series – Publication Date October 2010

ALEX MACKAY - TIME TRAVELLER

Morag Ramsey

Living in a block of flats that look across to Edinburgh Castle, Alex dreams of scaling the treacherous North Face of the rock on which it stands. He is a keen climber and, for a thirteen-year-old, very good. But the City of Edinburgh has long since forbidden the climb. Perhaps it is this dream that gets him chosen to travel back in time to a night in 1314 when he joins the band of desperate men under the Earl of Moray who defied the odds, climbed the rock and silently butchered every single English soldier in the Castle garrison. Unfortunately for Alex his journey back into the past has been organised by a rival outfit to SHARP. They are the Science Testing and Recording Programme (STRAP) and they are an unscrupulous lot: They don't care if the children they use in the twenty-first century get lost in the past or worse get killed.

ISBN: 978-09556169-9-0

Fifth in the series – Publication date November 2010

JO KELLY - TIME TRAVELLER

Sarah Garrett

Jo's extremely clever younger brother gets all the attention from her academic parents. They are world-renowned in their subjects and her father lectures at a prestigious college in Oxford. They have little understanding of Jo's warm personality and practical abilities. So, they would be amazed to learn that in her travels back in time, she arrives at Magdalen College, Christmas 1939 and meets, not only the famous academic and author C.S Lewis but the writer of The Trilogy as well. Her brother sings in the Magdalen College choir but it is Jo who gets to sing with the choir from top of the tower on the 1st May, a long-held college tradition, in the momentous year of 1945.

ISBN: 978-09564869-0-5

COMPETITIONS AND ACTIVITIES

Seven Arches Publishing often runs competitions for you to enter with prizes of book tokens, that can be spent in any bookshop, for solving puzzles or for a good illustration. Why not go to www.sevenarches-publishing.co.uk and check out whether there is competition or activity on its way based on one or other of our books. We often include the winning entries of our competitions, or the writing, poems or pictures that you send us in the next print run of the title.

CONTACT US

You are welcome to contact Seven Arches Publishing by:

Phone: 0161 4257642

Or

Email: admin@sevenarchespublishing.co.uk